Tont.

The Legend of Lilac Lane

CHRIS BRUNO

ITS BATMAN - DARK TO
START. JUT READ
EVERY WORD. OK?
IF ITS SHIT. I'll HAVE
SOME OTHER GOOD
STUFF FOR YOU SOON

♡ CHRIS

www.mccormackpublishing.com

Cover photo by Susan Munroe
www.susanmunroephoto.com

Cover design by: www.nd-designs.com

To:

Sr. Mary Howina Goofina
&
the Whomp du Flomp

"talk a minute"

Book One: The Man Called Claus

Table of Contents

Prologue..1
Chapter 1: Behold The Cold...5
Chapter 2: Born To Run..14
Chapter 3: Cape Clear..20
Chapter 4: Fruit of the Loom..27
Chapter 5: Speed is Your Friend...34
Chapter 6: When The Bough Breaks...................................40
Chapter 7: Rolling In The Deep..48
Chapter 8: The Flight of The Sleighter...............................56
Chapter 9: The Curse of the Suburbs..................................67
Chapter 10: Gee, Our Old LaSalle Ran Great......................77
Chapter 11: Rendezvous at The Old Guard..........................80
Chapter 12: *South* City...87
Chapter 13: The Riddle of Refueling...................................89

Prologue

"*SANTA! SANTA! SANTA!*" little Terrin Bailey cried. She released her grandmother's hand and burst through the white picket fence set up within The Shops At Tanforan like a filly charging through the starting gate at the racetrack which had once stood on this ground. She bounded across the AstroTurf path that led to the raised platform on which Santa's armchair was placed, ignoring the dour little man with the handle-bar mustache who attempted to slow her down.

"Umph!" Santa grunted, as Terrin landed on his bad leg with all her weight and spun to face him.

He had shaved off his beard this time and looked like the average imposter with a wiry, synthetic version connected to the wig from which hung. It covered his cheeks and hid his mouth and chin. His suit was a cheap velour two-piecer with the zipper of the coat hidden behind faux fur trim. His boots were comprised of plastic leggings with elastic stirrups to hold them tight to the cordovan thrift store penny loafers that had been spray-painted black for the occasion. He actually had a pillow stuffed in his coat as he had trouble maintaining his weight this fall— what with his travels to his suppliers world-wide.

"I WANT A FURBY BOOM AND AND A DOC MCSTUFFINS CHECK-UP CENTER AND A NERF REBELLE HEARTBREAKER BOW . . ."

Just Play Products, Santa thought. *I should take that meeting in the spring. And Hasbro, of course, crushing the Top Ten . . .*

"I WANT A BIG HUGS ELMO AND A FLUTTERBYE FLYING FAIRY DOLL, A LEAP PAD ULTRA AND SOMETHING NEW FOR

BARBIE!"

I'll eat the Tickle-Me overstock in the First World now or pay freight to the Third . . . and there's Barbour's uptick in EBITDA for you—why did I not invest?

"NO, WAIT! FORGET BARBIE! I WANT AN IPHONE!"

Big boob Barbie takes a dive . . . sales down 12 percent in July.

"I WANT AN IPHONE!"

God Almighty! At eight? An iPhone in the third grade?

Terrin looked straight into Santa's eyes. She leaned in, breathing eggnog on his face. "IT NEEDS TO BE THE IPHONE FIVE—THE FIVE-S!"

"Honey, what would you need that for?" he whispered to her, looking to her side but leaning in close as a priest might beside a confessional screen.

"IT HAS BETTER APPS THAN THE DROID!" "I don't know what you would need an app for," Santa said. *I rue the day that I bounced Stevie Jobs on my knee . . . . on that very knee.*

The little man at the fence with deep set eyes, a weathered face and a stare which might incinerate a child, caught Santa's gaze and touched his opposing wrist with a forefinger.

Yes, yes, of course—Time! I, who possess the most of all, seem never to have enough!

"Honey, I'm going to pick out the best thing for you to open for Christmas morning—it still needs to be a surprise."

"I WANT AN IPHONE!"

"I understand. But you may not get what you want, Terrin. I will ensure, however, you'll get what I think is best for you."

Terrin grabbed his beard. "DYLAN SAYS YOU'RE MADE UP!" She squinted her blue eyes and stared into his brown.

Santa looked to his left, and, seeing the photographer preoccupied, he sighed. He leaned closer. "Honey," Santa softened his voice, "I am of the opinion *we are all made up.*"

Terrin nodded, and lowered her eyes, still holding onto his beard.

"But are you *real?*" she whispered.

"Not so much anymore," Santa sighed. "But old age is like that."

Terrin nodded again, let go of his beard and touched the fur trim of coat.

"Now I'm sorry that Vanessa couldn't come with you today, but you let her know I was thinking about her and that I will have something nice picked out for her as well. And tell Mimi that these new candy canes"—he handed her one—"are sweetened with Stevia and that I'm sorry I contributed to her sweet tooth when she was your age—now you off you go—*wait!* Pose for your picture . . ."

FLASH!

" . . . and off you go! And you remember to stay on my nice list all year—OK?"

"OK," Terrin said, and slid down to her feet for her hot trot back to her grandmother.

"*H-H-Hold up!*" the little man said to the next family in line, lifting the tobacco-stained fingers of his left hand. "Santa's going to take a short break!"

Santa stood up and stretched out the arms that expanded the shoulders that had hoisted the weight of all the gifts given on one thousand Christmas Eves. He stepped off the platform, waving off help from his manservant.

"We're due in Kodiak," the little man said.

"I know," Santa said, clutching his foam-filled belly and following him behind the North Pole backdrop.

The pair walked quickly through a stream of shoppers to an unmarked door near an exit which led to the roof. The door was held open by a middle-aged security guard, who nodded as Santa passed. "Santa," he said.

"Robert," Santa grabbed his hand and held onto it tightly. "My best wishes to your family—and you tell those little boys '*I'm a comin'!*'"

"Will do," Robert said, containing a smile.

Santa winked at him and let go of his hand.

When the door was closed, Santa stripped out of his suit in the stairway and pulled off his wig and beard, exposing a stiff, all-white crew cut. He wore a white five o'clock shadow, like a light frost on his cheeks and chin. Santa kicked off his loafers and leggings and pulled on his black, hand-tooled boots that had been re-soled by the hides of a hundred head of cattle.

"We've got good cloud cover to the coast," the little man said. "And nightfall is nigh . . . but—"

"—but the reindeer are nervous." Santa completed his thought.

"All these people—*all awake* . . . ."

"I know," Santa said and slipped into his duster and flight cap once they had been handed to him. He pulled his calfskin gloves out of a pocket.

"Let's go."

The little man led the way up the stairs, checking back on Santa at each landing. Santa kept up with him three stairs back and felt some unacknowledged strain lifting from him when they reached the roof—it was when that first blast of moist bay air hit him. It kept San Bruno under a blanket of fog for most of the winter. A reindeer bellowed beyond them. Santa could feel the drumming of hooves on the gravel and tar paper roof. Corralled behind a beige fence that camouflaged the ventilation equipment from the traffic on Interstate 380, his current team could not contain their excitement in Santa's presence to get out of this place. A red light flashed. He looked out at the whitened airspace of the city and felt the fresh sea breeze which streamed over the gentle mountain range to the west.

"Time!" the little man called. "Time, Santa!"

"Yes, of course," Santa said. But he did not move from the spot, allowing the melancholy of the place to wash over him, the melancholy—yes—and the joy piercing a heart which kept time for all the world—the metronome of all humanity! The Greenwich Mean Time of Love! —there in his chest like a Grandfather Clock which ticked off centuries like minutes.

This holy ground, he thought. Millbrae to the South. South San Francisco to his North. The smell of See's Candy inland. And Guittard Chocolate toward the bay. It all came back to him—his past. Yes!

"TIME! SANTA! TIME!"

It all came back.

"TIME!"

That cold and desperate night so long ago when he learned who he was to become . . .

Chapter 1:
Behold the Cold

The soft undulation of snow in the forest belied the fury of the storm which had howled through it the night before. Hundred-year old trees lay uprooted upon beds of branches they broke when the earth exploded under the leverage of their straining trunks and they had crashed to the ground. All was entombed until spring in crystalline banks which rolled and dipped and curved around the heavily-laden trees that were still standing. The earth itself had been transformed into a frosted labyrinth of downed limbs, drifts, ditches and invisible ice patches. Nevertheless, one man made steady progress beneath a moon so bright at midnight that it seemed that the sun had simply frozen in place the day before and now shined weakly through a thick lens of ice.

The man leaned forward into his every step—now right, now left, now right—crunching through the fragile surface crust of snow which shone in blue-white light. With his gloved hands held behind his back, the man bent at the waist as he marched forward in a coat of thick, heavy wool. A fur-lined leather cap and a full black beard protected his head and cheeks.

He looked downward as he marched ahead, his labored breath a snow-storm in miniature before him. He wore heavy boots framed in small wood and gut snowshoes which left shallow, evenly-spaced shoeprints for miles behind.

As the man passed a stand of trees which stood ghostly in the hollow of the field, a ripple ran through the shadow of the tree nearest him. It was the suggestion of movement, as though the root of one tree had transmitted the oscillation of a bullwhip from its trunk through the snow.

As the man trudged on, this movement beneath the surface of things, this tunneling, emerged from the shadow of the trees, and sped across the distance between itself and the man and at an angle which guaranteed a collision. But the man, bent down, exhaling visibly, and staring down at his boots, could not see beside him as a burrow of snow erupted. A huge black and white dog, fully half the size of the man, burst into the air: its sharp teeth gleaming in the moonlight, its paws extended toward the sky. The well-muscled flanks of the beast shed its own weight in snow as it flew before the man and a white-tipped tail—almost half the length of the dog—nearly whipped the leather cap off the man with a manic swoosh of blackened fur.

The man did not so much as turn his head—that would require energy and he was conserving his. "Do you never tire?" he asked his dog.

The shepherd-mix curved back down toward the snow, meeting it rolled-over on its shoulders. It tumbled across the snowpack before sliding sideways upon its surface where it lay motionless except for its heaving chest and the one dark eye which followed the man as he neared.

He passed the dog and continued on when moments later the dog dove beside the man— a black and white flash at nearly eye-level—and then dove downward into a drift where it submerged like some unspent projectile. Only its hind quarters and tail visible from within the hole it had created in the snow.

In the smallest concession of affection, the man let out a small whistle of a single note, unclasped his hands behind him and held his left gloved hand to his side as he marched on. The dog burst from the small snowy chamber he had created and had caught up with him, fitting his muzzle in between the fingers and thumb for a short frozen stroke.

The pair reached a small ridge before them, and, recognizing it from their travels a year before, walked along side it until they came to woodland so dense that the ground below was barely dusted by snow, and the interlacing limbs of the trees all but blacked out the moonlight from above. The man unlaced his snowshoes and stepped out of them.

The dog came forward in this darkness, and then disappeared back into it except for the short white tuft of fur at the tip of his tail bobbing behind him. The dog kept a true line, stepping over roots, dodging the lean of a dying tree, snaking around fallen branches. He had picked up the scent that the man was now only beginning to smell: turf burning farther within the woods and meat which had been earlier roasted.

When the darkness was such that the man alone would be lost, the faintest glimmer of light appeared, a small glow that caused the dog to run ahead and the man to see his way again on his own. The man pulled off a glove and unbuttoned his coat, exposing the loosely-woven jumper beneath. He slipped one arm out and let the sling of a canvas bag slide off his shoulder where it had been hoisted throughout his journey.

He slipped the coat back on, holding the bag in his free arm and approached a small but sturdily-built home which rested on a foundation of interlocking stones. The cabin itself was made of hand-cut timbers, logs mostly, but the front door and an adjacent shed were fashioned with planks. A small window of stretched skin set high off the ground glowed from the light of a single oil lamp that burned within.

The heavy door of the cabin opened with a soft wooden moan as the man's dog pranced with joy at returning to the home while baring his teeth in anticipation of being censured for barreling inside. He let out a whimper, unsure what next to do. The man hushed the dog, who lowered his lips and sat.

But his tail swept at the ground, back and forth, back and forth.

A heavy dark drape hung before the opening. The man pulled this back and was immersed in the warmth of the home, the smells of the evening meal and the sounds of a half-dozen children sleeping soundly in a small loft above him. The man stepped inside, allowing the drape to fall behind him, and moved forward toward the soft glow of embers burning in a small hearth in the middle of the room.

The man bent over without making a sound and set the canvas bag down. He pulled on it slowly and allowed the contents to tumble out onto a rug of braided straw: dried sausage, a ball of royal blue yarn, a delicate bottle of perfumed water wrapped softly in cotton, a small wooden doll with a painted face, a metal bell with the clapper wound in yarn for travel, four dried apricots, a pair of dice, a rattle made from a Gourd and a clay figurine of a knight. He arranged the gifts quietly in an arc before the fire, and then rolled up the new, tightly-woven duck canvas bag and laid that before the hearth as well.

As he stood to go, the man, aware of the sounds around him, counted one less wind instrument in the symphony of breathing that had listened to since he had entered the home. One child was alert and holding his breath in the darkness. The man turned and looked upward into the loft where one head was lifted and all the others were still buried in down.

"Myrige Cristes Maesse," he said. *Merry Christmas.* He stepped toward the door, pulled back the drape, and exited the home, securing it against the cold. He bent down and laced up.

It was neither his dog nor the moonlight which guided the man out of the smoky grove; it was a new wind, and a speck of sharpness on his cheek—snow. He could feel the pin-pricks on his exposed flesh as the flakes threaded themselves between the trunks of the trees and found him—so minute a pelting. He was chilled slightly by the warmth of the home, but got into the rhythm of his march forward again.

Probably, just a flurry, he thought.

He looked up as the trees thinned and his path was easier to discern. It lead him to his snowshoes. He stepped in, laced them up and continued on. There on the ridge before him sat his dog, having chosen his own path to clear ground. The man let out a short whistle but the dog did not respond, remaining motionless as though frozen himself.

The flakes were light that fell between them but they were whipped up by the wind intermittently. The man did not want to climb the ridge—the ten or twelve steps upwards were fraught with danger, and the path back downwards could result in a fall. But the dog ignored another whistle and the call of his name in the wind, *"Lukan!"*

He then disappeared over the ridge.

God.

Begrudgingly, the man held his hands out to either side, balancing himself, and climbed up to what appeared to be a natural levee created from some previous outpouring of water from the other side. On the far side of the bank was a wide expanse of snow, miles across—as smooth as a meadow and completely unadorned with trees. Fifty yards ahead of him, upon this frozen field, his dog leapt skyward, barking a staccato greeting to his master and then running back and forth before him.

What do you smell?

Crossing the ridge, the man made his way down to the other side to the plain where the dog ran forward to greet him and then turned and, at a sprint, ran far ahead into the expanse.

His face began to numb—his cheeks.

Were they to reach the distant trees and discover nothing, with a mild wind he could return the way he came in little more than an hour.

Even if he were delayed, the coming dawn would hasten his return crossing and his passage home. A snowfall would not delay him.

A light snowfall.

Strung on his belt was a pouch of hardtack and a dried piece of fish. There also was a dented tin with a roasted turnip in it, half-eaten, and a folded paper with some spices. With moderate weather he could march an entire day with these provisions—even if he were to have to forego sleep. And if he could find shelter enough to melt some snow and boil some water for soup, he could endure for nearly two. He felt for the flint and striker hung around his neck. A quick jaunt across an ice field would be little trouble, he reasoned, and it would allow them to scout the way for their return trip the following year.

But half-way across the plain, the heavens unleashed a howling of winter winds that all but prevented his progress. He leaned into it, wondering what beckoned his dog so. If this was a turning of the weather, he might need to seek shelter back at that cabin in the woods.

Lightning illuminated the sky. And thunder exploded above him. .

"LUKAN!"

The dog would not return.

He lowered his head and marched on.

He approached what looked like an island on this plain, a steep uprising of earth, jagged to his left and right but sloping gently toward him in the center. The wind died down a little as he approached, blocked as it was by the trees, but snowflakes still spun around him. The violence of the storm had decimated the younger trees at the periphery of the island. Many had not survived the initial blast, and many more would die from the weight of the trees which had fallen upon them. He followed his dog's tracks upwards to a thinly-wooded area surrounding a glen of older trees. The man felt coolness at his throat as he looked up and surveyed shorn tree tops above; he lowered his gaze and was set to whistle for his dog when he saw him in a clearing, lit softly by snowfall as though the moon had just disintegrated and now fell to earth in illuminated ash.

Lightning lent a violet palette to things momentarily, and— *"BOOM!"*—thunder took it away.

The man stepped beneath the bowers above him and was surprised to see that his dog stood on cleanly-stamped earth, flattened smoothly and dusted in equal parts with straw and snow. Lukan's entire body wagged—

"BOOM!"

--he stood in the remnants of a home. The man opened his mouth to praise the dog, when he turned and saw the colossus of the tree that had crushed the house in the storm, uprooting it completely from its foundation, folding it over upon itself and knocking it aside from where it had once stood.

The sky went stroboscopic —*"BOOM! BOOM! BOOM!"*—and then it was dark again and quiet.

The man looked beyond the fallen tree. There in the ruptured roof of the flattened house, in the torn framework of timber and thatch, in a space barely large enough for one person, a mother cradled an infant within her night clothes and a small boy shivered beside her, clutching onto part of her gown.

Snow now fell like rain. Straight down upon them.

The weather had turned.

Before he could speak, the woman's husband stepped through the destruction beside them, too cold to shiver in the light tunic in which he had evidently slept. He had a straw mat in one hand, and a coil of rope in the other. He was expressionless, caught momentarily in freeze-frame.

"BOOM!"

Their eyes met with the realization that one of them tonight would die.

The man silenced his dog, who had begun to whimper, stepped around the mammoth root-ball of the tree that had demolished the house, took off his gloves and handed them to the woman with child. To the boy, he removed his lined leather cap and placed it on his head.

"BOOM! BOOM! BOOM!"

He unbuttoned his great coat, removed it and handed it to the man. He pulled his jumper off, moist with his perspiration, and draped it over the woman and child. He unfastened his belt with two carefully tied pouches and the small tin and this he gave to the boy as well. He bent down, unlaced his snow shoes, stepped out of them and kicked them toward the man.

He turned then, without looking back toward the family and walked back around the root-ball, nearly slipping as he stepped onto the floor that was once this family's home. He whistled for his dog, and, grabbing the bicep of either arm to embrace himself, he confronted the winds whistling through the small arbor under which he had just come, making his way carefully through the stand of trees.

The heavens detonated: *"BOOM! BOOM! BOOM! BOOM!"*

Then it was silent except for the sound of snow falling.

The man slipped down the icy ramp he had previously ascended, and tumbled end-over-end when his boots caught on the leading edge of the plain. He righted himself quickly, clapped the snow off his hands and slapped it off his arms and breeches. He followed his tracks as a searing coldness enveloped him.

The snow came down now in curtains upon him. And a wind began to rise.

The man's boots crashed through the surface of the snow and buried themselves a foot or more beneath it. They emerged twice their weight. His socks were now wet.

With every movement he grew colder. His shivering increased and soon he could not feel his legs—they moved, certainly, but only with the woodenness of remembered motion. The man searched in vain for his earlier tracks but as the swirling veil of snow before him obscured his view, even his own dog beside him was forced to stop and hide from the frozen crust that periodically lifted itself from the surface of the plain, and sliced through the air at ground level.

In his mind, the man was half-way across the wasteland on a straight line for the last home they had visited, but he had covered no more than a third of the distance when, snow-blind and stumbling, he turned sideways to the levy, unknowingly, and now would never reach it. His last hopeful thought was for his dog, who could turn at any moment and run with his back to the wind so as to receive from the family some shelter and a meager portion of food in light of how great a price his master had paid for the meal.

Still he trudged on: his eyes more closed than not—what was there to see but white? He willed each boot to arise from its snowy sinkhole—though he had now had no sensation in his feet—and willed them again and again to find another such temporary anchor for his body as it lurched forward. His hands gripped his arms as though he clung to the life-raft of his own torso. Were he to fall now, he would never arise. But as long as his legs worked, he believed, he may yet live.

A blast of wind lifted his head and almost threw him backwards, but he braced himself against it. He did not topple, but now neither could he move forward. The strength he had just expended remaining upright sapped his legs of what vitality they finally possessed.

He stood for a moment. Like some lost totem in an infinite field of ice.

But standing takes balance—even when one's legs are locked—and balance remains a possession of the living. So this, too, was stripped of him.

His knees buckled as he fell.

Oh, God.

He pivoted his arms at the elbow to catch his face as he hit the frozen surface crust. The impact took his breath away. He inhaled mostly snow, and was bent over as though praying. His hands were so cold and held a face so white that they seemed like ceramic bowls nesting within one another outside the smoke kitchen of his uncle's longhouse.

This was the first time the back of his neck was exposed to the cruelty of the wind. He did not think he could feel any colder, but this last place of warmth was stretched upon the guillotine of the plain, exposed as he was to the cutting edge of winter winds.

His mind was filled with the foolishness of his life, his silly outings, his ridiculous dreams of travel, and this manic quest to defeat the cruelty of the world in the dead of winter with the trifling of some ribbon and some lace.

When he realized that actually he was to be his own executioner, that he would embalm himself with ice at his every breath, that he would freeze from the inside out as his thoughts slowed and his heart cooled, he became glad for a moment—glad that an undertaking as ridiculous as his would be over, that folly would be slain by folly, foolishness by foolishness, stupidity by—

—there was a great rumbling beneath him, a shifting of seismic proportion—*"BOOM!"*—he fell straight down with the snow around him into a chamber his dog had dug beneath him. A hole desperately clawed from within.

Lukan waited there below, at the man's side, heaving and wild-eyed. He threw himself upon the man, and stretched out to his great length in a coat he would never loan to another. The dog kicked at the walls with powerful legs and the precarious snow pack at either side of the pit collapsed in upon them, burying them in a cocoon of icy insulation beneath the deadly wind above.

In a moment, the sharp edges outlining the chamber were softened.

In minutes, the depression above it was filled with the snowy dusting of so many whirlwinds.

By dawn, the hastily-dug tomb was empty.

There was no sign of the man or the dog.

And the morning was still and white.

Chapter 2:
Born To Run

Lukan begat Petran who begat Wolveram (the blue-eyed), who begat a litter with just two males, the black-faced shepherds, Tylo and Jone. These two were running at high speed through the forest, with Tylo, the younger, in the lead, and Jone, older by minutes, but heavier by a stone at his flank.

The crescent moon glowed behind a cloud cover at the horizon. This they aimed toward as they sped through thinning drifts of snow. Behind them at a quick gallop, a grey, speckled stallion pursued them. The man astride it rode bareback, in poor posture, leaning forward, his head bent over beside the horse's neck. His two hands gripped the mane of the horse and his legs flailed behind him as though belonging to the horse as some vestigial fins. His body rose and fell in time with the horse, and rose entirely off it sometimes when the horse was forced to leap so that it appeared that the man might fall off completely.

Jone could not keep up this pace. No animal could. He was the stronger of the pair, but slower. He looked back at the horse which was gaining on him.

The man had given away his two-wheeled sulky this time, and the colt that pulled it, and his coat, of course, and his boots and belt. He lay nearly unconscious on the back of his strongest horse, which would soon fail the man, because no animal could deliver him from his fate this time—he had ventured too far from home. And Jone, fading as he was, was himself moments away from being trampled if he did not slow up and let the horse finally pass.

Tylo lifted his head smelling water before his brother did—*running water*—and turned uphill beneath and between the evergreens which now were ever-white. Jone let him turn and listened for the horse to follow, then made his turn late, making his own path across a drift before falling into the horses tracks and attempting to keep up with them from behind.

Tylo looked nervous for the river he had smelled was deep enough in winter to continue to run. It was too wide to leap and it blocked their route home. He slowed, looking left for a narrowing of the stream, or a rock bridge to cross, but then saw up ahead a widening of the stream where the ice had formed and the current ran beneath. He could not slow down to test the ice, for fear exhaustion would take hold, so he ran past the first sheet of contiguous ice to a place where the ice looked thicker and they could run across it in seconds.

Tylo slowed, allowing the horse to study the ice sheet beside them, and when a bluff before them blocked their way forward and gentle slope ran down to the water's edge, Tylo made his turn toward the ice, increased his speed in descent and timed his leap across the ice so that his paws would touch the surface briefly just twice.

With one quick look behind him to insure the horse was following, Tylo made his jump. When his paws first hit, he heard a crack that would mean open water for a hoof. He tried to twist around to warn the horse, but this caused his weight to shift. He landed hard on a front paw, cracking the ice, which sent him end-over-end as the horse, seeing the spill, stopped hard and dug its front hooves in on the edge of the snowy bank. The horse threw its head down to put more weight behind its front hooves instead of above them.

The man did not look up as he was thrown from the horse, over its shoulders and toward the ice, tumbling through the air. The sickening report of something brittle breaking—either bone or ice—resounded in the countryside as the man hit the ice at the small of his back and then flattened out beyond the rupture in the ice he had just created. A new floe was let loose from its mooring downstream and now floated freely away.

Jone scrambled around the horse as it bolted back up the bank, nearly trampling him. It disappeared at full-speed into the forest as Jone stepped onto the ice, and, sensing no weakness yet, made his way toward the man, taking the path of a long-arc between him and the fissures in the ice he had created. His brother, Tylo, winded by the run and frightened by water lay on the far shore panting.

The man was on his side facing Tylo upstream—he did not appear to be breathing. His loose under-tunic was slightly pulled up from his waist, his brown breeches seemed thin for winter and one hose was torn at the ankle. Jone crept toward him, one paw at a time. When he peered over the man's ribs to look at his face, the man spun, caught the dog off-guard, and grabbed two fist-fulls of fur at the back of the dog's neck.

Jone ki-yied, ducked his head, and then threw it back and forth trying to dislodge the hands which held his fur with the very death-grip that had just held the horse's mane. He scrambled backwards on the ice, trying to pull away from the man, but felt something sharp beneath a back paw—a fissure!—and, sticking his claws into it, pushed back with all his might, jerking the man back with him while loosening a hand.

Jone's next attempt to jam a rear-ward paw into the ice submerged it into a liquid so cold it seemed to paralyze his body. He froze, unable to retreat, as the man grabbed another fist-full of fur: this time the shorter strands farther up his body. Jone tried to shake him off, but in doing so rocked the ice beneath him, breaking through the surface and plunging him into the stream.

Jone was submerged. He gnashed at the surface above him, but the man held him under—*and then he was gone!* Jone rose, gasping for air. He swung his head downstream and saw the man twist in the ice water, breaking the last bit of solid ice which held this floe fast. He then felt the current take them—the man, the ice, and him downstream as they obeyed the irresistible call of gravity which pulled them downward toward some distant sea.

The man was barely visible in the swift water, his head and shoulder at a height just higher than the chunks of ice they traveled with; but in the turbulent water and at the falls, Jone could glimpse a leg or arm or piece of clothing. He fought with all four paws to keep his head up to get a breath, enduring the vise-like hold the cold water had on his chest.

Save for a solitary stroke of the man's arm, it appeared that the man had completely surrendered to the current. He ceased to struggle.

There was a pooling of water in front of Jone, where huge boulders projected upward from within the earth, damming the water slightly before sending it to the right in a jog where it cascaded downward in a turbulent froth. Jone dug madly with his paws, clawing and pulling and pushing his way through the water though the cold had robbed him of so much strength. He buried his muzzle halfway into the water before him as he leaned his shoulders forward and churned the liquid ice with all the muscles yet firing in his chest.

He felt something solid beneath a rear paw and kicked at it hard. Then a front paw hit gravel, then all four touched down together and he propelled himself upward out of the water and onto a sleek, steep rock bereft of snow. Jone scrambled up the rock and climbed upward until he came to a flat spot overlooking the pool from which he had emerged. He shook off the water but still felt immersed in it.

Jone peered into the mists rising up from the cascading water and, to his horror, saw a fifteen foot drop beyond them. He turned his gaze forward and saw the man floating lifeless where the pounding water of the falls had dug out the riverbed deep enough to allow calmer waters to create a pool below.

Jone circled once upon the rock, whimpered slightly, took a step and then flung himself off the top of the rock into the abyss, his four legs cycling through the biting winter air. He hit the water on his side, and descended to an eery depth he had never been before.

He paddled upward, bursting from the depths to steal a succession of breaths in a quicksand of slush. He spied the man lying face-down before him in the water, paddled toward him and clamped onto the man's arm with his teeth. Jone paddled to a depression in the bank. He turned when he got a foothold, bit down hard on the man's arm again and dragged him half-way out of the water.

The man coughed. And then vomited up ice water. And then dragged himself out of the water on his arms onto the snow-covered beach. He coughed again.

God, help me.

He turned over on his back, so cold he no longer shivered. He stared up through the tree limbs overhanging the river and at the diffusion of light which barely lit the clouds above him. Suddenly, his peripheral vision darkened—as though night had fallen again on two opposing horizons. He felt the world closing in upon him—a great weight pressing in upon his body—and vomited again. A bile which had no warmth.

"No!" he cried out, lifting one arm to the sky before he dropped into unconsciousness.

Hypothermia claimed all the sensations in his body and then returned with a new set moments later, belonging to a completely different person; one who was warm, at ease and calm.

Jone shook off on the beach, colder than he had ever been in his life, and came alongside the man. He lay down beside him, shivering, but the man's flesh was so cold he leaned away.

The man felt giddy and carefree. He knew this was the end. He was too cold to feel any colder. Too cold to register the lack of warmth. Or even to shiver. Hypothermia would claim his consciousness again and again until it would simply not give it back. He needed warmth now. He needed food. There could be no further flight to shelter. He needed a fire. But he was too weak to get up to dig through the snow for fuel. And the flint and striker hung round his neck were worthless without it.

He regarded his dog, who could not stay much longer beside him, but would have to scout out some shelter in the forest or run to keep warm. He then looked upward again just as a lone owl spiraled above him beyond the tree tops, gliding on unseen winds, ignorant of the forest floor it did not touch, rivers that did not block its progress and a snowstorm which never piled snow high enough to threaten its roost. The man watched the owl, forgetting his impending doom and admired the breadth of its wings, the majesty of its feathered head and a heft so impressive compared to all other birds...

How could something that big get aloft?

He shuddered for a moment—this last, uncontrollable shakedown of his limbs. And was gratified to see that his breath was still visible, that his lungs were still warm enough to heat the winter air as it entered and then left his chest. This, too, would stop.

He registered a tingling on his exposed forearms. His dog bites did not bleed.

He looked up again and watched as the owl seemed intent on circling above him instead of landing. It was though it was observing the man as the man was observing it.

It could not be envying me, the man thought, *in the manner I envy it.*

But still the owl circled.

The man scanned the branches above the tree that grew from a carve-out in the river bank—its branches skirted just above the bank itself. He pushed himself up on his elbows, tilting, it seemed, the very axis of the earth in the process. The man steadied himself.

He looked to the sky. It was as though the owl was caught on an updraft from the river and rode the wind effortlessly. But there was no updraft lifting the owl, the man knew, only fear. There was something in the tree the owl did not want the man to find. Something made of dry twigs and pine needles in which its eggs were warming.

Something very close to him.

Something he could climb to.

Chapter 3:
Cape Clear

Jone begat Geoffrey who sired a litter in which all but one puppy drowned. The lone survivor was female, Cleire, who, despite being slighter than the cousins with whom she ran—

and much slower—had a sense of smell which surpassed that of any dog that the man had ever kept. But such a sense worked against Cleire on this day as the effluence the man trudged towards on a brisk spring morning caused Cleire to whimper long before the man had ever caught wind of it himself. Manure means livestock. Livestock means wolves.

He was marching along on a road rarely used in the woods, rutted from former use, but too soggy in early spring to be of much use to anyone except himself. A man on horseback would have avoided it and no wagon could pass. But the man walked along at its side at a pace admirable given the large sheaf of straw he carried on his back. He walked bent forward, in the pose he used in winter when shielding himself from the cold. He wore brown breeches, high leather boots with leggings exposed and a short black coat buttoned at the waist but left open at his chest and throat. A light yellow scarf was knotted at his throat and billowed before him, obscuring the tunic he wore underneath. A simple red sock hat covered his head.

Cleire ran ahead of the man, far ahead, scouting out danger or fun in the long spring grass. The woodlands thinned and the road straightened out for lack of trees to divert its path. The ground grew hard under the man's feet where it had been baked by the sun, and the stench increased in pungency with each new waft. As the man topped a knoll, the source of the smell and the reason for the straw appeared in the distance. The spring run-off had cleaned out the livestock pens on a distant slope at a time when the value of one's *fiefdom* and the meaning of the word was merely the amount of cattle one possessed. The waste of the animals, which had yet to be determined to be any value, ran down the hill to a small gully. When full, this gully poured toward a crossroads beyond where four homes stood sentry. Three of these were abandoned with caved-in roofs and missing doors where the spring thaw seeped across sodden thresholds and made a cesspool of each home. Only the fourth remained intact.

Here, where the pungent pool crossed the road, the man untied the straw and tossed mounds of it in the stagnant water. He stepped from one soggy lump to another until he tossed the last of it farther than he thought he could jump. He swung his arms, leapt across the muck, bounded off his last precarious pile and jumped to the exposed foundation of the wall which ran beside the house and beneath it, providing him a ledge upon which to balance. He held onto the house itself and was able to enter the front door without getting wet.

The place was filled with barrels of grain, bottles of spirits (dressed for travel in woven corsets), brass implements of an earlier age, statuary small enough to have withstood vandalism but not theft, an ornately-carved mantel pulled out of a much larger house and leaning against a wall, two sets of delicate chairs, enough cutlery and cookware to furnish the three abandoned homes outside, and oil paintings of the revered or the forgotten. All of it was stacked up for inspection and sale. The overriding smell of the place was of the tar-baths the proprietor soaked in, not of the manure.

"We both know the more money I entrust to you, the faster you shall flee from me and the farther you shall run," the proprietor said. He was an old man who spoke at the rear of the shop beyond a tall wooden table stacked with manuscripts. He addressed the younger of the two men on the ground floor of the home. "There will be no return for me," the old man said, running a dry, crusted hand over an equally dry scalp which allowed only the slightest adornment of white hair above his ears. "We both know this."

The young man wore a bronze-colored cloth coat over a white blouse with a large limp collar. He did not return the old man's gaze.

"And the tobacco you have taken from the chest is yours, but heed these words—*do not smoke it with a stranger.*" The old man extended an unsteady forefinger toward the young man who tucked his blonde hair behind both ears. "Leave this place and my welcome with it."

The young man turned, and tracked muck back across the worn, oiled wood floor which was for sale itself and installed correctly by a joiner to show why it might be bought. He left the room without meeting the eyes of the other two visitors.

"Come," the old man said to the other young man in the room. "Approach me."

The dark-haired youth kept his head bowed as he came forward. He spoke softly to the old man and was dressed in a black coat too heavy for the sunlight of the day.

"Yes," the old man agreed with what the young man told him. "I have bought from Eisenhauer. I know him. He has spoken of you— yes!"

The young man spoke in tones too low to hear from the front of the shop.

"That is a difficult journey even at this time of year, my son. Not impossible. But arduous. Why do you go?"

The old man closed his eyes as he listened. Again, he rubbed his scalp as though sanding down his head with the calluses of old hands lest hair begin to grow again.

"They need tradesmen there, yes," he said.

The dark-haired youth spoke softly again.

"Yes, of course, they produce beautiful work, but, so, so fragile— this cannot interest me. Look into my eyes. Look directly in them." The old man stared intently into the young man's eyes for a moment and then closed them. "Tell me the name you were given at birth. It is different from what you are called now, isn't it?"

The young man responded.

"The full name. As it was written in the Church register." The old man kept his eyes closed. "Mmm."

A silence overtook the room.

"What do you think would interest me in those lands?"

The young man's response was short.

"Ha! I buy those things only when they arrive in my shop. I cannot commission so difficult a journey to enrich the thieves who poach them. No, let me think. Let me think."

The old man pulled out a ledger from below the tall table, laid it out flat on top of the manuscripts and flipped through its pages. "Some linens," he finally said. "A tapestry, perhaps. Find the most expensive item in an open stall, from a man who does not sell such things for a living. Determine that the value is what he says it is—*listen to me*—determine the value is what he says it is. Return the following day and offer him half. Return the day thereafter and offer him less. Each day do the same. Continue until he shouts for you to stay away. Then leave him with his thoughts for a day, return, and show him half—*show him*—and then he will let go of what he loves."

The young man nodded.

"Find the most expensive method to send it, find the most guarded caravan. Be persistent. Tell them your master only entrusts them with the shipment. If it costs more to send than you then possess, tell them to collect double the debt from me. Listen to my words—listen to them and heed—and I will pay for your travel."

The old man reached below the counter again.

"These are for you," the old man said, as he counted out six large, bright coins. "Bring along half the food you need—only half. But eat in secret and accept what meals are offered. Do not travel until the new moon and then only travel alone or with single men. There will be nothing for you to learn from your companions. Keep your thoughts to yourself. Be mindful only of your safety and of your eventual arrival. Do not bathe. Do not sleep alone. Do not observe the Sabbath. Each day you are to make progress. Never travel at night. You will find your way."

The dark haired youth responded softly and nodded.

"Take these coins now, but return to me on the evening before you are to travel and repeat to me all that I have told you."

The dark-haired youth, placed the money in a coin purse hung around his neck, bowed, made a quiet word of parting and walked out the room.

"Come," the old man said to his final visitor. "Come closer to me—come." The old man held his hands out before him in greeting. "Have you been here before?"

"I know you," said the man as he pulled off his red stocking cap.

"Then let me consider you closely." The old man said.

The man stepped closer.

The old man closed his eyes and then opened them. "You cannot fool me. You are your father's son!"

"All men are, but you mistake me for my heir."

"What? Come here—come! Give me your hands."

They were offered and then held tightly

"Nicholas?" the old man asked. "Is it you?"

"I am myself."

"*What?*" the old man exclaimed. He gripped Nicholas's hands tighter and pulled him closer across the table. "How could this happen?"

"I know of no way for it to not."

"Lend me your cheek," the old man said and placed a mitt of aged flesh against the thick black whiskers of Nicholas's beard. "How is it that you hold time hostage?"

"I do not hold time at all."

"Then why does it pass through you but carry me along with it?"

"It is my work, Lucian," he called the old man by name. "It makes a gift of the present without presenting me a bill for the past."

"Then what do you need of me?" the old man asked. "What can a man with no future provide?"

"I must..." Nicholas hesitated. "*I must be released from this earth*...to do my work." He rubbed the worn wooden counter between them as he spoke. "*I must fly across it!*"

"Give me your hands again." Lucian said. "Give me your hands." He took them in his, held them together in his own, as though praying, and then peeled them apart. He placed them palms-down on the counter. He laid his own hands upon them.

"You will fly, young Claus, *you will fly!* I see this clearly—but you must find the beast unburdened by its brethren. Do you understand? Find the animal as alone as you."

"But I need them *now!*"

"But they are not here for you now—I am. And I say you must travel through time to find them."

"I could die this winter for want of them!"

"It is not the earth that beckons you, Nicholas—it is the sky!"

"But you have no idea the price I pay for each new year!"

"Perhaps not, but I long to possess that currency!"

"You speak in riddles, old man!"

"Riddles prevent us from learning too much too soon." Lucian responded. "They are meant only for our memory—and yours is to stretch across time as the heavens bend across this earth."

"Can you not understand me?"

"You curse, Nicholas, is that no one ever will. But you will understand us all—our dreams, our hopes, our needs."

"But I do not even understand myself!"

"Your identity will be disclosed to you. When you come into your power, Nicholas, you will spend your years like days."

"But it's the nights that scare me, Lucian, *the nights!*—there is one in winter which is my trial."

"You will always find new life in darkness, Nicholas," the old man said. "You will always find new life. Consider that the longest book ever printed is only illuminated two pages at a time—the coming darkness will always contains unread riches for you."

"You tell me nothing, old man!" Nicholas cried. He looked around the shop. "You talk in circles and tell me I am to see some animal fly!"

"I will tell you this, young Claus," Lucian said. "These beasts will rise only for you. You will not *see* them fly. You will *make* them fly."

"I, who leap puddles today, am to take a team aloft? Nicholas asked.

"This fog you are in will lift—it will reveal your path."

"Paths are carved in dirt, Lucian!" Nicholas cried. "Or in manure!"

"You are to be unbound, young Claus! You are to be unbound."

"MY NAME IS NICHOLAS!"

"But you are to be called The Claus—you who are to name will be named."

Nicholas grabbed Lucian's hand as though to speak. But it was too much for him. He shook his head.

"Remember this old fool, Claus, when a father you become!"

"Am I to have children?"

"More than you can imagine," Lucian said. "And your stores will make a mockery of this one." He pointed to his inventory.

"But I learned so much as your apprentice."

"But what you are to teach others, you did not learn from me."

"I learned everything from you!"

"No, your conscience is your guide. And I now am merely pupil."

"No!"

"All soon shall study you. All will seek you out!"

"No!"

"I can only give you what I have!" the old man cried. "Take it all, take everything you see, take it with you before I, too, am flooded out and swept away."

"No," Nicholas said. "This is yours."

"Use it in your work!"

"No, Lucian!"

"What use is any of this to me? What good is it anyway? Take it, young Claus! Take it all!"

"No."

"Then take one thing of mine! Take something of mine to carry when you're unbound!"

Nicholas looked around the room once more, and saw with new eyes a short velvet cape. Crimson was the color—as would befit a king. It had ermine trim and a gold cord at the neck.

"Yes!" the old man said, following his gaze. "I will be your cape!"

"Then you *are* a fool, old man!"

"I shall fly beside thee!"

Nicholas grabbed the old man's hands and brought them to his lips without kissing them. He released them, turned with dry boots, and walked toward the cape.

"Godspeed, good Claus!" the old man cried.

Klaus took the deep red garment from where it was hung and was gone.

"Godspeed!"

Chapter 4:
Fruit of the Loom

Nicholas bent down, grabbed another fully-loaded canvas sack and hefted it onto his shoulder. Adjusting the load on his back, he trudged through the deepest part of the drift where his team of two horses had just pulled his empty sleigh.

"Umph!" he grunted, as he heaved the bag over the back of the sleigh and rested for a moment. He watched as his dog, Julep, the blonde, returned from her short outing.

Nicholas retraced his steps and grabbed the second of his seven bags in order to fill the sleigh back up for the third time this evening. Had his load been as light as he had expected by this time of night, his horses could have hit the dune at a gallop and the sleigh would have sailed over the drift, but he found the large farmhouse in the glen empty this year and the bridge beyond it was out, forcing him now into the deepest part of the woods with his sleigh still heavily-loaded with gifts.

He could stash a few bags amidst the trees in the hope to make better time, but it would cause him to have to double-back when he ran out of gifts.

Julep nipped at his trouser leg as he hefted the last bag over his shoulder. He ignored her, marched thirty-seven steps in deep snow to the sleigh and threw the bag into the back. He climbed in, found his flask of sweet, black tea, uncorked it and raised it to his lips. One cool drop fell out. He stowed the flask, picked up the reins and, while making a clicking sound with his tongue, urged Starlight and Starbright, his twin chocolate Palominos, forward.

The weather was mild on this night. The snow he traveled through had been compacted by a week of sun and wind and weight. Where he traveled on level ground through the trees, the team made good time, but he did not recognize any landmarks in the hinterland—usually he only returned from his annual trip along this route, and usually was not fully-awake when he did.

The cloud cover broke enough for Orion's belt to become clearly visible. He almost stopped to pull out his map, but thought the better of it and let his horses run. He didn't actually know if there were any homes along this route. The river he followed protected the best farmland on the far side and it was a long journey to the next bridge. Nearly an hour passed in silence, and Nicholas was getting cold from inactivity.

Julep leapt out of the sleigh and ran alongside. She lifted her muzzle toward Nicholas: "Wah-wah-wah!" She whined. It was something more expressive than a growl, but not so determined as a bark. Nicholas slapped his thigh and the dog leapt back up into the sleigh. She threw her front paws up on his thigh.

"What?" said Nicholas. "What do you want to tell me?"

"Wah-wah-wah!" She whined.

"Oh, I am sure it is very, very important," Nicholas said.

The pair and their team passed a stand of enormous trees and were illuminated as though it were high noon on a summer's day. Beams of light so bright that they were blinding fell upon them. Nicholas slowed the team as they came around a bend in the road. He shielded his eyes. There in a clearing where the river turned inward to meet a wharf along the shore was a great two-story house illuminated for what he assumed was a tremendous holiday party being held within. Twelve windows in the top floor and twelve windows below it bathed the snow-swept land in light.

"What wealth!" Nicholas mused.

As they came closer, Nicholas could hear dancing! Dancing! A hundred revelers or more slapping their hands in unison to music they drowned out with the pounding of their heels! Perhaps the recipients of his gifts tonight were all assembled together! Perhaps he could present their gifts all at once! He touched his salt and pepper beard, wishing it were more neatly groomed and adjusted his cap, frayed now from so many seasons of traveling. He wished for something finer.

"Ow-wooooo!" said Julep.

As Nicholas's team came closer, he could see clearly that they were at the rear of the great home. There was no proper entrance on this side and no teams of horses, or sleighs either. Nor did he see a stable or hitching post.

"KLACKETY-KLACKETY-KLACK!"

"It must be formal dancing," Nicholas spoke to his dog and his horses, "Some great family is holding court . . . but on such a sacred night?"

And then Nicholas realized it—there was no path leading to either side of the home. There was no walkway. No garden. It was a solid block of a building devoid of ornament—just those twelve casements above and twelve casements below. And that noise:

"KLACKETY-KLACKETY-KLACK!"

What sort of home is this?

Nicholas tied off his reins, climbed down out of the sleigh and walked beside his horses. He stroked Starbright with an open hand, and with Julep beside him, advanced through the snow toward the casement nearest him.

"KLACKETY-KLACKETY-KLACK!"

The building was much larger than it appeared. It did not have the proportions of a proper home. From the road it looked as though he could just peek into the casement on the first floor, but as he approached the building, it seemed to grow with his every step. As he came closer he could see that he might not be able to peer into the building even on tip-toe. Nicholas stomped up a short drift piled against the building which could provide him an unobstructed view of the interior.

"KLACKETY-KLACKETY-KLACK!"

He grabbed some snow off the window ledge, melted it in his hand and smeared it on the oiled parchment pulled taught across the casement—it burst upon his touch. He made a mental note to bring a stained glass replacement next year. But since it was now torn, he peeked in.

"MACHINES!" Nicholas cried, so startled was he at the sight. "MACHINES!"

"KLACKETY-KLACKETY-KLACK!"

They were looms, actually. A hundred of them, stretched from one side of the great room to the other, operating with such speed Nicholas could not be sure what he was seeing: spools of thread spinning, scores of shuttles automatically being thrown back and forth above the woven cloth.

"KLACKETY-KLACKETY-KLACK!"

"Good, God!" Nicholas said. He tore open more of the parchment. It was brittle and gave easily. He looked back at his team, thought of the time, but tore the parchment off entirely, wondering if any people were in the building at all. He climbed through, turned around with his hands on the sill and let himself down to the manufacturing floor below.

"KLACKETY-KLACKETY-KLACK!"

Nicholas stepped nearer to the loom closest to him, bent over, and sought the source of its power. *Water-wheel driven?* As he stood up, the machine stopped.

Nicholas looked through the heddles to identify the contrivance that started or stopped it, but saw none. He stepped to the right to look more closely at its twin in operation. This machine stopped. Nicholas looked back to the first machine. Now the one on the other side of it ceased its operation.

"KLACKETY-KLACKETY-KLACK!"

Nicholas saw a door on the far wall to his right, down the length of the building. He began to walk toward it. As he did, each loom he passed stopped working in turn, as did all those in the row behind it, causing the rhythmic percussion of the room to miss a beat.

"KLACKETY-KLACK!"

Nicholas began to run as he sensed some motion in the aisle beyond the first row of looms.

"KLACKETY-KLACK!"

It's an animal!

"KLACKETY-KLACK!"

A pack of them!

"KLACKETY-KLACK!"

The machines are all shutting down!

"KLACKETY!"

The creatures are racing to the door from beneath the machines!

"KLACKETY!"

The door is so close!

"KLACK!"

BUT THERE IS NO LATCH ON THIS SIDE!

"KLACK!"

BUT THERE IS A SMALLER DOOR WITHIN IT . . . AT EYE LEVEL!

Nicholas drove his fist through this smaller door, breaking it apart, and driving his arm through to his shoulder. He reached down on the other side of it until he found a latch which he threw as he looked back at the machines.

THEY ARE PEOPLE! HUNDREDS OF THEM! SMALL, FURIOUS, DIRTY LITTLE PEOPLE!

Nicholas pushed the door open with his shoulder, extracted his arm, and ran across the frozen ground to his team, whistling for a fast start. But it was too late! The team and the sleigh were swarmed—ant-like— by scores of strong, fast-moving little people. They threw themselves upon the horses which could not run for the weight which now hung off their harnesses. The miniature people leapt into the sleigh, tearing the wrapping off the gifts and throwing them high in the air behind them where they were caught by the ever-advancing horde.

Nicholas made it to the bench in his sleigh, but his boots were held firm by the first little people to reach him. His legs were held firm by the next group which leapt upon the shoulders of their brethren. His hands were bound at his sides and his arms were gripped by a hundred fingers. He was being swallowed up by a growing pyramid of small people!

"WHAT DO YOU WANT?" Nicholas cried, his hands pinned to his sides.

"WHAT DO YOU WANT?" came the response, although the inflection was wrong.

"I ONLY SOUGHT TO SEE THE MACHINES!" Nicholas cried.

"I ONLY SOUGHT TO SEE THE MACHINES!" the little people spoke in a cascade in the forest.

"I AM NICHOLAS!" Nicholas cried.

"I AM NICHOLAS!" came the response.

Nicholas was silent for a moment and so were they.

"I AM NOT YOUR MASTER!" he said.

"I AM NOT YOUR MASTER!" the little people responded.

"We will let you go now!" Nicholas said.

"We will let you go now!" came the response, though Nicholas was not let go.

A little man with a dirty, unkempt beard raced toward the sleigh and leapt upon should after shoulder until he was at eye-level with Nicholas.

He raised his hand as a package was thrown through the air and he caught it with just a sideways glance at its trajectory. The little man tore open the package exposing Nicholas's own brown bread.

"SCHWEE!" the little man said, holding the bread up.

"Schwee," Nicholas repeated.

The little man nodded. He took a piece of bread with blackened fingers and ate it in front of Nicholas with teeth nearly as dark. He swallowed, smiled, and touched his lips, his throat and stomach in quick succession. "Wee!" he said.

"Wee," Nicholas responded.

The little man took another piece of bread again, and patted his stomach with his free hand, "Schwee-wee!"

"Schwee-wee," Nicholas responded and the pyramid of small people collapsed in upon itself. They gathered in clusters and exchanged Nicholas's gifts with each other, sharing the items of food they had found among them while they continued to search among the wrapping paper, cargo nets and packaging material for anything they may have overlooked.

Nicholas's dog, Julep, watched the scene from the forest. Her ears were up. She did not move.

Nicholas stepped from the bench in the sleigh to the ground where he brought the reins of his team around to the front of the horses who were still being held in place by a group of little people. He asked them, "Schwee-wee?"

They nodded and let go of the horses.

Nicholas whispered to his horses whose eyes seemed as strangers to their sockets. He led them around to the road. As the sleigh pivoted on its rails, the first small duffel was thrown into the back, then a second, then a box of food, and then a bucket brigade of belongings amassed a heap in the rear of the sleigh greater than the gifts that had previously been stored there.

Nicholas continued walking while his team could still pull the weight of the sleigh. When he looked behind him, he saw that the little people now were wrapped in layers of work clothes and were following him in long lines behind the sleigh. He extended his gait as he made for the main road, but found the little people had kept up in double-time. Finally, he stopped.

"Schwee-wee!" he said. "Good bread! I understand."

"Good bread!" came the response. "I understand."

"You go back to work!" Nicholas called.

The small people did not respond en masse this time. But one small woman stepped out of line and spoke to the group. "YOU GO BACK TO WORK, YOU VICIOUS LITTLE PYGMY, OR YOU'LL NEVER SEE YOUR BABY AGAIN!"

She stepped back in line. But another woman stepped out. She, too, turned to address the group.

"YOU'LL LOSE A FINGER OFF THE OTHER HAND, TOO," she cried. "IF YOU DON'T GET THIS MACHINE RUNNING BY DAWN!"

Julep came in close to Nicholas. He bent down and stroked her on the muzzle.

A little man stepped up beside the second woman

"BLEED ON THIS LINEN AGAIN, YOU LITTLE MONKEY, AND I'll GIVE YOU THE CAGE!"

The forest was silent as Nicholas considered the throng of small people lined up behind his sleigh.

"COME WITHME!" he called.

The little people did not respond this time.

But they followed.

They followed.

Chapter 5:
Speed is Your Friend

The silver ribbon glistened in the cold night air as the present to which it was attached sailed over the high garden wall and two outstretched white-gloved hands caught it deftly and pulled it down to nestle against the thick crimson coat that matched the cape that Nicholas wore. He leapt across one flagstone to the other, both of which rocked beneath his weight as he landed upon them.

"To your left," an elf said, holding the front door open and handing Nicholas a stocking packed with homemade holiday treats.

Nicholas ducked beneath a low inner doorway, set the present and the stocking before the hearth. In three steps, he was back out the door, and into the sleigh just as one elf on board snapped the reins, sending them rocketing down the narrow moonlit lane.

"Hands!" A second elf, twin to the first, asked

Nicholas held out his gloved hands, palms up.

The elf pulled the soiled right glove off, placed it in a pouch on his smock and replaced it quickly with a clean identical version. "Schaefer family in…TIME?"

"Forty Seconds!" came an elf in the rear of the sleigh.

"Schaefer family in forty seconds—two daughters, Marta and Katrina, jumper for one, clogs for the other, spinning tops, candy canes—BITE!" He held out a piece of shortbread for Nicholas. "Spinning tops, candy canes, and two spools of yarn for their grandmamma—TIME?"

"IN TEN!"

"In ten seconds: gravel path, unshoveled but firm…"

"EIGHT"

"…duck before entering—high door, but low tree limb before it…"

"SIX!"

"…hit your boots on the grate and avoid the runner inside the door…"

"FOUR!"

"…sharp right and place the presents beneath the tree…"

"The what?" Nicholas asked.

"TWO!"

"…the *tree!* I'll explain later!—*GO!*"

The elf slapped him on the butt as Nicholas leaped out.

"TIME?"

"TWELVE SECONDS TO LAUNCH…TEN!"

* * *

"Sir," the elf spoke softly. "Are you sleeping?"

Nicholas was awake in the darkness, fully-dressed. "No," he said.

"The goats," he said. "They're ready."

"Take me to them," Nicholas said, arising in darkness. He was led by one small light through his room at the abandoned monastery which served as his home.

He followed the elf outside on a moonless night when a chill cut through clothing warmed by the drowsy twitching that masqueraded as sleep. Deep through the forest in a clearing, small oil lamps burned on the sides of great oaks illuminating a group of elves harnessing a mature male goat with lines which extended upward to the darkened branches above.

"This way," the elf said.

He led Nicholas to the far side of a shorn tree which glowed from lamps shining on either side of it.

Nicholas put a foot on the lowest rung of a ladder dovetailed into the trunk and grabbed another at eye-level, testing to see if both could hold his weight.

"Very good," he said, approving the craftsmanship—the steps as sturdy as the limbs on the tree. "May I?"

"Please."

Nicholas ascended the tree in concert with the last goat who was being hoisted up by the elves on the ground.

"HEAVE!" cried an elf with a clipboard before him.

"HO!" responded a team of elves, who jerked the suspended goat three feet up in the air.

"HEAVE!" came the command again.

"HO!" responded the hoisters.

Nicholas climbed up, keeping pace with the goat who—at a height of thirty feet— was now level with nine others. These five pairs of two hung in a harness strung across two mighty trees like long johns come-to-life on a clothesline.

Nicholas climbed up through a platform to a lightweight sleigh suspended from a catwalk above and fastened to the harness which held the goats. Oil lamps burned behind hurricane glass at all four corners.

"Are you sure you're ready?" an elf asked.

Nicholas nodded and stepped into the sleigh, which wobbled beneath the lines from which it was suspended. He grabbed onto the bulkhead for support and stared over the side at the last goat struggling in its harness as the elf in charge of him attempted to un-foul his lines. Above him four elves were stretched out on their bellies on rope-bridge with knifes prepared to sever the tethers holding the sleigh.

Nicholas slid onto the bench and grabbed his reins with one hand, a bullwhip with the other.

"ALL CLEAR!" came the call when the last goat was in place.

An elf leaned into the sleigh, "Say the word, sir!"

Nicholas looked out across the goats suspended in their harnesses and at the ten elves above them all eyeing him—poised to saw through the rope to which they were each assigned..

"BBBLLEEEAAAATTTTTT!" called one goat.

A gentle stream of urine from one sparkled in the lamp light as it descended to the ground dividing itself up into golden drops.

Nicholas stood up uneasily, handed the whip to the attendant elf and accepted his help back onto the platform. "This isn't going to work."

"No," the elf said. "I didn't think so either."

* * *

"TEN SECONDS TO LAUNCH!"

The horses had to be held in place with the reins.

"EIGHT!"

Nicholas appeared at the doorway of the home and leapt across a patch of ice before it.

"SIX!"

He landed in the sinkholes in the snow he made on the way in, jumped in and out of each boot-step—his knees high, his arms pumping.

"FOUR!"

He held onto his cap as he approached the sleigh.

"TWO!"

Nicholas leapt into it; the reins were snapped and the sleigh bolted across the front yard, skidding on the frosted ground cover and straightening out enough to clear the twin stone pillars which demarcated the drive.

"Hands!" the attending elf called.

Nicholas held out his gloves.

"Fine."

"Bite!" the elf stuff a chunk of fruitcake in Nicholas's mouth.

Nicholas bit down and shook his head. "Not good!" he said, his cheeks full.

"We'll re-gift it. TIME?"

"THIRTY SECONDS TO TRANSFER!"

"Are you sure you're ready for this, sir?"

"Hmm!" Nicholas nodded and grimaced as he swallowed.

"Once you start, there is no going back!"

"I…" Nicholas cleared his throat. "I understand."

"TWENTY SECONDS!"

"We've stripped down the new sleigh completely—it's held together with dog-spit and nose hair. The harnesses on the horses are thin, but strong. The horses themselves you'll recognize--young, strong and full of dreams. When you come to the 'Y' where you veer right for Wagner's, bear left instead. Downed trees on either side of the lane will prevent the team from going off course . . ."

"TEN SECONDS!"

Two young black horses came abreast with gleaming silver hardware in their harnesses pulling an unloaded, unpainted sleigh. The elf controlling them tied off the reins, and prepared to leap in Nicholas's sleigh as Nicholas leapt in his.

"Once you crest the hill there is no going back."

"EIGHT!"

"Remember—speed is your friend!"

"SIX!"

"This pair will want to run, so let them!"

"FOUR!"

"Don't be concerned about steering, just let them loose on the descent!"

"TWO!"

"If you have any questions, ask me later—*GO!*" the elf cried as Nicholas hurdled into the new sleigh. He tumbled, recovered, grabbed the reins, and lifted a hand in a farewell salute. He steered left at the 'Y' and drove his team down the lane.

"Yah!" Nicholas bellowed, cracking a whip in the air behind the horses. "Yah!" he commanded again as he snapped the reins for greater speed.

The team crested the snowy ridge that marked the high point of this lane—the fallen trees and uprooted stumps preventing any deviation from their course.

Nicholas whipped the reins and urged the young stallions on, convinced he had never traveled faster in a sleigh. He caught sight of the ramp before them, camouflaged with a thick layer of snow. They would hit it at the end of this sharp decline and sail thirty or forty yards to a meadow beyond the hollow below.

The horses charged downward in unison, stretching outward to their full length when they, too, caught sight of the ramp. They threw their front hooves out in emergency braking, lowered their heads and allowed the sleigh to flip forward at their harnesses, flinging Nicholas forward as though shot from a catapult as they skidded to a stop.

Nicholas sailed through the air with his arms flailing and legs kicking. Momentarily, he appeared to be flying . . . really, truly flying—but the uncontrolled landing buried him deep in the fresh snow of the hollow. His cheeks burned despite the cold and he hoped he might suffocate quickly before he was found.

Then his dogs were upon him.

* * *

"No!" Nicholas said. "No more." He refused the flask of tea and pulled the blanket up over his head to shield himself from the sun. He and his Delivery Administrator, Thelonius, were crouched up on the back of the sleigh on a long, smooth ride home through virgin snow in the forest.

"Five thirty-three, five thirty-four, five thirty-five—FIVE HUNDRED AND THIRTY-SIX HOMES!" Thelonius announced staring at his clipboard. He was crouched up against Nicholas. "That's pretty good!"

"Think so?"

"Twenty percent increase since last year."

"It still doesn't seem like a lot."

"Yes, but that's about two thousand children . . . if you include those last families."

"The last families?"

"The kids were already awake—but the parents distracted them until we left."

"Does that count?"

"Sure—you have to keep the kids in the dark about how this all works until they're old enough to understand."

"They're so gullible," Nicholas said. "They'll believe anything you tell them."

"Yes, but not the parents," Thelonius said. "And you know what they say about you, don't you—the townspeople?"

"What?" Nicholas asked.

"They say you're a saint."

Nicholas was silent for a moment. "They underestimate me," he said.

Chapter 6:
When the Bough Breaks

"My lovely," Santa whispered quietly to himself. He spied the sleeping girl curled up in quilt before the weak glow of the hearth of the house he had just entered. He placed a gently-wrapped wooden doll with an exposed painted face and auburn hair beside her, supine, so she would see it as soon she opened her eyes.

He considered the girl in slumber, comparing the elegance of her features to those he had crafted in the doll.

An animal bellowed. And then again. He did not recognize the sound.

Santa stood up and looking through the doorway he had just come, witnessed the purple bruising of morning at the horizon as it collided into night..

Santa moved without a sound through the narrow, low-ceiling home left vacant during grazing seasons. He exited the house, closed the door and walked past his sleigh and the single elf within it preparing for the last delivery this year. Santa crunched through surface snow to a hastily-constructed corral on the far side of the house that had been erected beneath the eaves of it and a meager stone granary. He saw among the two-dozen pens, a pair of animals that he presumed were caribou, but they were smaller than caribou although seemingly full-grown. They had enormous antlers with two separate groups of points, a smaller set leaning forward above their eyes, but a larger set, like velvet palm fronds set high on "L"-shaped tines far above their heads.

"Tch-tch," Santa made a clicking noise with his tongue.

The larger of the two, the bull, wore a light coat and a mantle of blond fur around his great neck which crested at his shoulders. He turned his head slightly at the sound, but remained unmoved.

Santa stepped closer. The smaller of the two—the cow— grunted and averted her eyes, but stood rooted beside her mate.

"Time, Santa, time . . ." called the elf.

Santa lifted a hand slowly toward the pair. The bull sniffed him through generous nostrils and studied Santa from beneath a crown of antlers.

"Time, please, Santa . . . *time.*" The elf appeared at Santa's side and touched his sleeve.

"Yes, yes . . ." said Santa, "of course." Santa spoke a word of farewell to the pair, but they looked back at him expressionless. The hulking bull turned toward his mate. She scratched at the ground and marked a stripe on the winter white canvas with the cleft of a split hoof.

"IF YOU PLEASE, SANTA, *TIME! TIME! TIME!*" The elf pulled at Santa with all his might.

"Yes, of course . . ." Santa trotted back to the sleigh and jumped on the running board as it pulled away from the encampment.

* * *

Two fresh teams of horses pulling an empty sleigh blasted through the forest on a course determined largely by the unguided steeds who received infrequent direction from the twin elves bouncing above and before the bench on which they tried to sit. One elf lost his grip on the reins of the runaway team and was bounced into the back of the sleigh, entangling him in the cargo nets stored there. The other released the reins entirely and took refuge beneath the bench.

The horses charged across powdered snow and through trees festooned in white until they came to a well-beaten path leading to the abandoned monastery of their home.

Seeing the team approach, Santa stepped through the vestibule doorway to beckon the horses. They trotted toward him as Santa held out his hands to them—the promise of a sweet fruit in winter and a quick firm hello with his palms. He stepped around them to the sleigh.

"What is the good word?" he asked.

"Not a single good one to you from that animal trader," said Mandelke, the elf up front, who did not bother to rise from his resting place. "He will not sell those animals to you."

"Then he will give them to me for free!" Santa said, sore in the back from his deliveries the day before.

"He said he would keep those animals forever."

"Forever?" Santa asked. "I redefine the word."

"He said he doesn't care who you are."

Santa held out his hand. "Come," he said, motioning the pair to step out of the sleigh. "Soon he shall."

* * *

Night had come when Santa escaped into his workshop. He stocked the small stove with hand-carved toys that would never make it into production. In the resulting blaze, the twin sister to the wooden doll he had left with the little girl stared at him from her shelf. He picked her up, cradled her in his arms and warmed her face with the whisper of his breath. Santa held his cheek to hers until the coldness of her complexion disappeared. He kissed the doll, stroked her auburn hair, and straightened the plain cotton shift that she wore in preparation for next season's finery. He returned her to the shelf above his workbench.

That night at the animal trader's encampment, the man's daughter took her doll to bed with her as she had the night before and held her tightly as she slept.

Her eyes moved rapidly when light from a crescent moon, sweeping the land for its darker half, touched her curtains with illuminated longing, and provided the necessary light to project terrible dreams.

"Aaaa!!" the little girl screamed, as the weariness which retains sleep was overthrown by a fear that needs no rest.

"Aaaa!!" she screamed again and then threw off her bedding, leapt to the floor, ran down the short packed earth hall of her home. She burst open the door to the storeroom in which her father slept and launched herself into his arms before he was able to register that the screams he had heard in his own dreams were real.

"Poppa! Poppa! Poppa!" she cried, throwing her arms around his neck and laying her head on the curling blond hair of his chest where his bedclothes buttoned.

"I was an acorn, Poppa! An acorn!"

"Catch your breath, Sana," he said. "Catch your breath."

"I was an acorn, Poppa! An acorn and I fell to the earth, fell far to the earth, fell from a limb of tree so tall you could not see the top of it from the ground. I fell to earth soaked up in the soil—in rich, black, steaming soil all mixed together like something baking, like chocolate and cinnamon. I swam around in it until I was warm and it covered me and it fed me and then I began to grow. I emerged into sunlight. I was streaked with rain. I could see my mother, Poppa—the tree! The tree! She was my mother far above. I reached for her; I lifted a single sprout, and I grew, Poppa! I grew!"

"Of course, you grew!" Her father said, and stroked her hair.

"I grew so tall, so broad, so much bigger than I am today. I grew and grew and grew and stretched out my limbs above me and beside me and nearly hugged the sun I was so high. And people came to me because as I protected them from the heat, and they could hide from the sun beneath me."

"Take your time, honey" he said. "Catch your breath."

"But some of the things they did in the shadows, Poppa, were not nice! Some of the things they did were mean. I could hear them fight. I could hear them fight beneath me. They tore the trees down on either side of me and sharpened the wood to make spears and stocks and rods. They used the wood to attack each other or imprison each other. They built a gallows with the wood. They killed people and then they built coffins and buried dead men like bad seeds into the earth and planted wooden crosses upon them when they did not grow. And then, Poppa, these people came for me! With wooden axe handles and wooden shovel handles, they marched toward me!—oh, Poppa!" She turned her head upwards to look to him and wept on his chest.

"There now," he stroked her hair. "There now. You're fine, Sana. You're with me. I will always protect you."

"But it seemed so real, Poppa! It seemed so real! It was all about wood—what men do with it! Wood, Poppa! Just wood! From a tree!"

"Dreams are like that. There are bad ones. but there are good ones, too. Why don't you just think back to what you liked about being a tree? Tell me the best part. Let's think only of that."

"There was no best part."

"Well, you told me there was—when you were growing upward toward the sun."

"Yes," Sana said. "I liked that. I liked growing upward and creating shade. There was a moment when two of your animals approached me. I could feel their weight upon my roots and the nibbling of grass at my trunk—I couldn't see them, but I could feel them, I could sense them, and I was happy that I could comfort them because they bore such great peace."

The father was silent for a moment. "My animals?" he said. "Mine? Which two were those?"

"Hmm?" she said, as played with the silken tie of his nightclothes.

"Which two animals of mine did you dream of?"

"Why…the ones that belong to the little men, of course!" she replied.

The man pushed her aside and sat up in bed.

Moonlight had just touched his curtains.

* * *

Santa lifted the lid of the box set out for him by the elves. Within it were luminescent glass globes, perfectly round. They possessed just the smallest of points on the bottom and a small fluted opening at the top where a gold crown held onto a looped metal hanger. On the inside of the lid was a message which read, "FOR THE TREE!"

He gently picked up two of the globes, sky-blue and orange, and walked across the darkened choir loft to a bare fir tree twice his height and hung the heavy orbs on the end of opposing branches. The limbs drooped downward from the weight. but they looked very pretty set off by the green needles. He added another pair and then another until he had hung them all.

Santa stepped back to admire the display.

"BOOM!" the orange one crashed to the wooden floor, releasing the limb to boomerang the into the one above.

"BOOM!" a silver globe fell and struck another in descent.

"BOOM! BOOM! BOOM! BOOM!" They all came down and bounced upon the floor echoing throughout the chapel below and rolling at Santa's feet without breaking.

Santa looked down into his own miniature, multi-colored spherical reflection in each and said to himself, "Guess I need a bigger tree!"

He took out his notebook to remind himself of this, but found on the first blank page a note written in bold elfin writing:

Noah knew
Never nay-

Say a sooth
Seemed insane
By the base.

He smiled, flipped this page over and found another note:

Dream of down
Drayman, do,
Willing wing
Where now wells
Hooves and heels.

He laughed to himself, read it again, looked back at the last page and read that again, too. He turned the page and found one more note.

Beg the beam-
Basking bays
Faithful flight.
Fetlocks fail
With no will.

"Beam-basking bays?" Santa thought to himself.

He stared at the sagging roof above him in the choir loft and the rafters that extended from the beam in the center and extended to either side. He studied its whorls and knots and the whitish water-stains that had raised the grain in places. Santa's eyes followed the beam to the wall at the rear of the choir loft and down the flaking, discolored wall towards a sooty stained-glass window, which illuminated Nicholas's laboratory in mottled dimness. A chisel-edged piece of blue glass had fallen out of its came during the previous winter and now a shaft of sunlight streamed in from the aperture, defined narrowly in the loft by the dust Santa set into motion with his every movement.

"The beam!" Santa said, discovering how solidly the sunlight extended across the loft. He walked toward the window, rose on his tiptoes as best as he could in his slippers and, closing his weaker eye, squinted through the rent in the tunic of some lesser-known saint. He looked out across the treetops, down at the monastery grounds and saw the animal trader's two animals tethered under a tree in front of the chapel.

"THEY'RE HERE!" he cried. "Ho! Ho!" Santa threw his notebook down and bounded down the circular stairway two and three steps at a time, bursting out into the courtyard.

Backing away from the shoots on which they had been nibbling, the pair regarded him in silence. He slowly crouched down and made some clicking noises with his tongue. The bull lifted his head for a moment, gazed at Santa and then resumed nibbling beneath the pawed ground for wisps of rye uncovered by his cloven hoof. Santa whistled to them in notes that attracted his dogs, but they did not respond.

"Can you get them to talk?" He asked Thelonius, who was tending them.

"I don't know."

"You don't know?" Santa asked.

"No."

"What do I pay you for, Theolonius?"

"Ah…well, you don't actually pay me, Santa."

"Well," Santa paused for a moment, and then stood up. "Now you know why."

* * *

"Anything?" a younger elf asked as he entered the new animal pen. He was stroking a beard that wasn't there and couldn't grow.

The elder elf was in the middle of the pen, on his haunches, holding out some moss to the new animals. "Schwee?" he offered. "Schwee?"

"Anything?" the young elf asked again.

"Maybe, methinks … maybe—" the elder elf said. "The female—this dote—ignores us well when the male is alert, but when he dozes—and doze he does—she does not fancy loneliness. She'll keep us at her flank, appears more interested in moss than men, but when she feeds she'll turn her head and stare me down."

"And?"

"And I twitch as her sleeping steed twitches—like so." The elf snapped his head twice to the right, made a clicking sound and then blinked.

"And?"

"And then she continues to feed!"

"That's it? "

"That's what?"

"That's all you've got?"

"That's better than you ever did with the goats."

"The goats were daft! They just make noise! They don't speak a language of their own so they're not going to learn one of ours!"

"The goats talk loud enough with their eyes. I will still make progress on the likes of those!"

"Like Santa cares!"

"They may still fly!"

"In your dreams!

"Santa has his sights set on these antlerope!"

"Antlerope?"

"It's now their official name—it's kind of like 'antelope,' but it's not, and they both have antlers and they don't mind to be tethered—*antlerope!"*

"I supposed you made that up?"

"If you are jealous of the genius of its authorship, then, yes, you can direct your spite towards me."

"That's as stupid as your squirrel-powered umbrella!"

"If you're referring to the *GyRoDent*, it will soon propel Santa to the rooftops unaided."

"What about the *thunk-thunk-thunk* of squirrels getting flung against the inside of the barn during your time-trials?"

"Progress has its costs."

"Tell that to the squirrels!"

"Nevertheless, it will succeed. And Santa's name for these animals will never catch on."

"What? *Reindeer?"*

"Far too difficult to spell."

Chapter 7:
Rolling In The Deep

"That's a funny looking goat," the lead dog said in Schwee-wee.

"These aren't goats," Thelonius responded. "They're reindeer. Great Flying Reindeer."

"Oh, c'mon," said the lead dog with half an ear chewed off. "Reindeer can't fly." He suddenly bit his left flank where a flea had just pierced his skin.

"No, *dogs* can't fly." Thelonius answered. "Reindeer *can*. I suggest you remove yourselves at once before you learn how sharp their antlers are."

The dogs darted their eyes toward the racks of antlers above each reindeer. They slunk off into the woods.

The smaller of the reindeer—they called her Louise—turned toward Thelonius, "Are you sure we can fly?"

"Positive," said Thelonius. "No doubt about it." He adjusted her harness and proceeded with the next drill. "Haven't you seen *the book?*"

"The book?" Louise asked.

"Yes," Thelonius said. "*The Great Flying Reindeer of the North!*" He pretended not to look at her, though he watched her reaction.

"The Great . . . ?"

"Oh, come on, Louise! Don't play coy. If we have a copy, surely you and James grew up with one."

"I don't know what you're talking about."

"The Great Flying Reindeer of the North? The elves all know it

by heart!"

Louise shook her antlers.

"Our copy is nearly falling to pieces—come, let's find it!" Thelonius led her out of the proving grounds and back to the monastery, where in a converted stable stuffed to the rafters with over-size, hand-bound books, Thelonius pulled out a heavy, fragile, nearly-portrait-sized book.

"It's just about reindeer?" Louise asked.

"It's a history of reindeer flight," Theolonius said, laying the book on a table and attempting to open to the first pages which were glued together from the wet ink of this morning's printing. He flipped quickly to the middle of the book. "Yes, here we are!"

Louise moved a little closer.

"I think this is the part when your ancestors first flew across the Baltic," he tapped the darkened watercolor of a team of reindeer in flight. "Oh, it was a terrible storm they endured."

"Really?"

"Of course!" Theolonius turned the page, but the whole book nearly came with him.

Louise nosed closer. "It smells kind of fresh."

"We had to touch up some of the colors—it was faded with age."

"Oh, yes. Yes, I understand."

"I think we have a more sturdy copy for you and James to look at—it will be ready...er...I will have it brought down from storage for you tomorrow."

* * *

Beginning on the following evening, in the smithy's shop next to the stalls where they were kept, James and Louise listened to fantastic stories of travel and daring in the firelight of the coal-fed blast furnace. They studied artful renderings of their legendary kin, and imagined what it would be like to fly together, soaring over great mountain ranges and storming blackened seas.

"Louise," James said, after the elves had left one night and they snuggled beside each other in the dark. "I want to fly! I want to fly for Santa!"

"Don't be silly, James," Louise said. "Reindeer can't fly! They can't really!"

"But I feel it, Louise! I feel it within me!"

"What you feel is impetuousness, James! You have no wings! No feathers! Nothing to keep you aloft!"

"But, I could make the sun shine from pure desire!"

"Silly," she nuzzled him. "You're just a reindeer."

"There is a higher love, Louise! A higher love! I can feel it! I can feel it on Christmas Eve! I feel it in Santa. I want to reach it for him, Louise! I want to fly!"

"Hmm," she snuggled closer to him. "I will follow you to the very sun you desire!"

"Will you?" James turned to her in the darkness.

"I will," she said. "Or to the moon!"

* * *

As Christmas approached that year and as the reindeer's coats were being brushed out before bedtime, Santa appeared before them and told them that their gift this year was ready for them now. The pair followed him into the darkness of the monastery grounds, lit only by the swinging light of his lantern, and then to the chapel where they stepped into the vestibule. He led them up the circular stairway to the choir loft where he stood before a curtain, which covered the view of the chapel below.

"Are you ready," asked Santa?

"Uh-huh!" James and Louise nodded.

Santa threw back the curtain and the two of them cried out in amazement, their eyes of gold widening in disbelief. Far below them on the chapel floor, painstakingly crafted in miniature, were the 1,000 homes to which they would deliver this year. Wisps of smoke emanated from miniature chimneys; soft flickering light illuminated tiny frosted windows; whole forests were duplicated tree-by-tree, snow-drift by snow-drift. Even the intended path they would take in just a few weeks on this night was carved minutely in the snow, hoof prints and all.

"This is what it looks like from above," Santa said.

James's heart beat now to a faster tempo. He looked over the pony wall of the choir loft and wanted desperately to hurdle it.

* * *

On Christmas Eve, Santa launched a boat of considerable size—

Goede Vrouw—named after the girl who did not grey as she awaited a century for Santa's first kiss. He would use the boat as a floating warehouse, which allowed his elves to restock the sleigh at designated sites throughout the night.

He planned to carry provisions for another a hundred homes along the coast, which the crew of the boat should be able to reach by sailing out the mouth of the river in order to meet up with the sleigh by the seaside.

They made good time that night when they finally had reached the sea at 4 AM where their boat was waiting for them along a rotting pier. The team took on their last load of presents, spun on the salt-water slickened planks and rode past deserted storefronts and warehouses, up a cobbled street to a crowd of weather-beaten homes that looked out to the sea.

"There's one," called Santa. "The pink door."

He hopped from the sleigh, held his hands out high and caught a tin of wrapped biscuits thrown to him from deep within the sleigh. He tried the door. It opened and he disappeared inside, emerging a moment later empty-handed. Santa jogged down the street, his reindeer trotting beside him.

"This one!" he called, grabbing a gift thrown to him and adding another new home to their inventory of believers. Santa continued like this from house-to-house over the next hour, sensing which house to visit and which to ignore. They emptied the sleigh quickly as the elves made a crude map of the roads they had taken and the houses they had visited. The sky grew lighter, and the houses grew farther and farther apart, until it seemed as though they had, indeed, delivered a gift to every believer on the coast.

Two gifts, though, remained in the sleigh. Climbing back in, Santa ordered the reindeer up one road and then down another. He double-backed and rode along the last two roads they had visited with his eyes closed and his hands covering his face. In his mind, he raced through each home he had previously entered and visualized each room and the family members asleep in his or her bed. He scanned the houses that he had not delivered to, and plumbed the hearts of the residents of these, searching intently for a trace of belief, but found none.

Santa ordered the reindeer to the coast for signs of their boat. A light rain began to fall on them and the elves in the back of the sleigh huddled beneath package netting and drifted off to sleep. Santa looked at his map again and at the two gifts in the sleigh.

Perhaps, just a mistake. But a pang of regret stabbed his heart. "No," he said. "They're undelivered."

Santa looked out to sea. Against an ever-lightening horizon was a small dark patch of land. "They are for two boys," he said. "Brothers . . . named after kings."

The two reindeer looked out to sea and saw what he stared at.

"That must be seven miles out!" cried James.

Santa brought his gloved hands together like the pages of a book. He considered them, raised them to his face and covered it with them.

"But where is our boat," asked Louise? "Where are our elves?"

Santa did not answer.

"But what are we to do?" James turned and asked Santa.

Still he would not speak.

"Surely, you can't expect us to fly that distance over water," James cried, "when we've never even flown before over land!"

Santa did not speak and would not look up. He sat motionless on the sleigh. His head remained bent. His face remained covered.

James looked over at Louise who hung her head down toward the ground. James hung his head down, too, and a great grief came over him. His eyes welled up with tears as he staggered away from the sea, pulling Louise beside him. He stumbled up the hill they had just come down.

"Reindeer can't fly," He thought, picturing the mean dogs from the woods. *"Reindeer can't fly."*

James imagined the two young boys asleep in their beds and their waking up on the greatest morning of the year with no gifts, and tears dripped down the fur of his muzzle. He reached the top of the hill and looked back down through the light rain at the stone quay and the harbor and beyond it to the sea itself and the dark finger of land on the horizon.

"Reindeer can't fly," he told himself. "Reindeer can't fly."

But then a terrible ferocity gripped his heart— *"Reindeer can't fly,"* he cried, *"But I can!"* James whipped the sleigh with a start and bolted down the rough cobbled hill with a new-found might which knew no fear.

His every muscle exploded in desire. He stretched his forelegs out as far as they could go and pulled the earth greedily toward him. He dug into the stones themselves, ripping the cobbles from the ground with his hooves, and clawing his way faster, and faster, and faster to the harbor. His lungs burned from the effort. He breathed in enough oxygen for a whole herd of his kind, expelling it with a roar, and sucking in twice as much with his very next breath. James ran faster than he ever had in his life, carrying Louise beside him who was valiant in her attempt to keep up—her hooves barely touched the ground as they sped downward toward the water.

James gobbled up the ground before him and shot down the quay in furious release of his need—*his right!*--to leave the earth! The water flashed and twinkled in the muted colors of morning, as he catapulted himself and Louise from the bank, his forelegs extended *upward, upward, upward* toward the lightening sky.

But no sooner had the sleigh become airborne than it began to sink, pulling them downward from behind. James clawed desperately for flight, digging into the air for some hoof-hold, some earth, some hope. His head up and eyes wild, he lunged for the last bit of open space given to him in descent.

Santa pulled hard on the reins to port. "Come about!" He called.

James leaned toward port, just as the rear of the sleigh smacked the liquid ice of the Atlantic. James reared up as his hindquarters were seized by its freezing grip.

He pounded the water with his hooves and struggled to get one last gasp of air as he sank. The seawater boiled with his effort. He flailed at the water, unwilling to yield his life in its coldness, digging, fighting, pulling, spitting, bucking his head back and forth as he finally submerged beneath it, expelling the burning contents of his lungs with a bubbled cry of defiance. His legs slowed, his brain ached and he believed himself to be drowning as his body convulsed in cold-water shock.

Santa yanked hard on his reins, snapping James's head back barely above the waterline. James sucked in the air feverishly and dug into the water again with unsure strength.

"ARISE!" Santa roared from the partially-submerged sleigh. He pulled hard on the reins. *"ARIIIISE!"*

James rose upward on command like some great, newly-discovered creature of the deep, his well-muscled legs cycling gracefully in icy Atlantic waters.

His mate beside him was a study in symmetry as she herself rose from the water: breathing, reaching, pulling in unison with James, their coats glistening in the pre-dawn air. They ran through the water without effort, their musculature rippling between their skeleton and skin, their antlers and arctic coats dripping with the brine of their rebirth. The pair lifted their heads in unison and they flew! —flew just above the water, their hooves and the rails of the sleigh slicing through the tops of the highest waves. They flew at a speed two or three times that of what they were capable of on land and were able to turn the craft with just the slightest lean to either port or starboard.

The elves, who were awakened by the crash in the water, finally untangled themselves from the package netting in the hold of the sleigh and, struggling for a foothold, stood up and peered over the edge of the bulkhead. They were stunned at what they saw: a frosted blue-black ocean speeding by below them.

"HURRAY!" they screamed and danced about. "HURRAY FOR SANTA!" They cried. *"HURRAY FOR JAMES AND LOUISE! HURRAY FOR US! HURRAY FOR THE WHOLE WIDE WORLD!"*

They danced about in the back of the sleigh, kissing and laughing and pushing each other over into a heap and then peering over the edge once more and losing their caps in the slipstream. *"HURRAY! HURRAY! HURRAY!"*

Santa pulled back on the reins and slowed the pair back to land speed as they approached the island. Without touching the ground, they slid off the water and up over a small berm on the coast. They flew just above the wild grasses and the scrub, and came to a narrow dirt road, where Santa signaled again for greater speed. They shot forward again across the island, following the contours of the earth, up a long steep hill beside stones fences and small cottages that dotted a great sloping shelf of land. Santa pulled back on the reins and slowed the reindeer down until their hooves and the sleigh rails touched the ground again. They made a sharp turn to the left and stopped outside a one-story light-colored house with a short dry-stone fence beside it and plaster shed off to the side. The elves handed Santa the two gifts from the back of the sleigh. He slipped into the front yard and disappeared along the far side of the house.

Trying to recover a breath he did not realize he had lost, Santa paused at the kitchen door before sneaking in. The house was warm, and smelled of the cakes that were still in their pans on the cupboard. As his eyes adjusted to the darkness, he saw a young woman, the mother of the boys, asleep before a coal fire glowing with a sparkle through the grate. Santa laid the boys' gifts at her feet and regarded her—she was taller than most women, with long, angular features. Her hair was a golden orange, curling wildly along her neck and shoulders. The stains of potters' clay were evident in the fingernails of her long, thin hands. Santa turned his head and listened for sounds of the boys who were asleep in the loft above him—they would be waking before long. Santa reached into his pocket and took out a short flat box containing the present he was to give Mamma Claus later in the day—an alabaster hair comb. He took out the comb and laid it on the lap of the young woman and, bending down, pressed his lips against the top of her head.

The boys stirred above and Santa snuck out of the room. He tiptoed into the kitchen and out the door—but thinking the better of it, he stepped back in and dug two fingers deep into the cake pan nearest him, pulling out a large hunk of moist soda bread. He closed the door without a sound and trotted back out to the road, splitting the bread in half to feed James and Louise. He kissed James on the fur above his nose and scratched him between the ears.

"I knew you were the one," he said.

Chapter 8:
The Flight of The Sleighter

"HATCH COVERS!" the senior pilot, Foster, cried through a woolen muffler frozen across his face. Their sleigh was coming in heavy to the Claus Compound at the North Pole with canisters of Indian dye packed to the gunwales. They were flying threes sleighs back on the right side in a "V" pattern, descending from their cruising altitude of 10,000 feet. The sky was clear at that altitude, but a puffy blanket of cotton balls hid the pole from them.

"SECURE!" his co-pilot cried through a black, ice-encrusted turtle-neck unfurled upward above his nose.

"SLEIGH-RAILS?"

The co-pilot leaned over the side of the sleigh on his side holding onto the safety bar that blocked a premature and painful exit from the bench. "CLEAR!" he cried.

"WHIPPLE-TREE?"

The co-pilot leaned forward over the bulkhead and inspected the whipple-tree and equalizing bar of the sleigh. "CHECK!"

"LANDING LIGHTS?"

The co-pilot threw a switch on the bulkhead of the sleigh: "ACTIVATED!"

"REINDEER?"

"REINDEER?" the co-pilot looked over at Foster as the lead sleigh in formation wagged its sleigh rails and broke left. The first sleigh on that side pulled in behind him and the first sleigh on the opposing side pulled in single-file in the third position as the sleighs in this squadron stacked up one behind the other to land.

"REINDEER!" Foster exclaimed. *"CHECK THE REINDEER!"*

"THE REINDEER?"

"YES!'

"REINDEER BUTTOCK—CHECK!"

"I CAN WASH YOU OUT RIGHT HERE AND NOW FOR INSUBORDINATION!"

"BUT IT'S A STUPID QUESTION!"

"IT'S ON THE CHECKLIST!"

"OK! I CHECKED THEM!" The co-pilot looked out over the team. "THEY APPEAR TO BE ATTACHED TO THE SLEIGH!"

"GOOD!" Foster cried, handing the younger elf the reins, "NOW YOU TAKE THE HELM!"

"OK—HEY! WHERE ARE YOU GOING?"

"DOWN BELOW TO LUBRICATE THE KINGPIN IN CASE YOU SCREW UP THIS LANDING!"

"CAN I HAVE A SIP OF THE LUBRICANT, TOO?"

"WELL...ONLY SO THAT YOU WILL BE ABLE TO DISCERN KINGPIN LUBRICANT BY TASTE IF REQUIRED TO!"

"OK!"

"JUST A SIP NOW!"

"TASTES LIKE SCHNAPPS!"

"EVERYONE SAYS THAT!"

"IS IT DIFFERENT?"

"OF COURSE IT'S DIFFERENT!"

"WHAT MAKES IT DIFFERENT?

'THE BACKWASH!"

The cotton puff blanket blew past them as they descended quickly through it.

"OH, MY GOD!" the co-pilot cried out.

Over two thousand sleighs were descending through the clouds flying on parallel paths toward three dozen illuminated runways on the far end of the warehouse district of the Claus Complex.

"NEVER BEEN HERE BEFORE?"

"ONLY SEEN IT IN PICTURES!"

"HA! THEY DON'T PHOTOGRAPH THE GOOD STUFF!"

They bled their airspeed as they passed diagonally over Runway 22 B on which they were to land, keeping their place in the stair-step landing pattern.

"I HATE THIS PART!" cried Foster.

"WHAT PART?"

"THE TAXIING TAKES FOREVER AROUND HERE!"

"SO?"

"WE'RE YOU PLANNING TO SLEEP PRIOR TO OUR NEXT FLIGHT?"

"I WAS HOPING!"

"NOT GOING TO HAPPEN!"

"GEEZ."

"WELL, WATCH THIS—EASIEST WAY TO GET SOME SHUT-EYE AT THE POLE!" Foster grabbed the reins and telegraphed something tightly to the pilot reindeer. He waited patiently for the response and then handed the reins back.

"WHAT DID YOU DO?"

"WATCH PINKSTON CAREFULLY!   HE'S GOING TO THROW A SHOE!"

"THROW A SHOE?? HOW CAN HE DO THAT?"

"CRACKED HOOF! WATCH THIS!"

The pilot reindeer of the sleigh rose slightly in his harness shook a foreleg and a flash of titanium caught in the landing lights spun downward in an arc. The whole sleigh began to shake as the team fell out of rhythm. It dove hard to the right, wobbling in response to the lack of reindeer control and fell away from the echelon.

"OH, MY GOD!" the co-pilot screamed. "WHAT DO WE DO?"

"HOLD ON!" Foster stood up, grabbed the white knuckle bar and lifted a hand as though he was bull-riding in order to signal to the other sleigh pilots above that he was OK.

The sleigh began to buck as the front half of the team stretched out in a dive and the rear half auto-rotated in resigned acceptance of what appeared to be imminent disaster.

"YOU TAKE THE REINS!" the co-pilot cried.

"GIVE THEM HERE!" Foster cried. "WEEEEEEEE!"

The sleigh rocked side-to-side in descent and rattled the canisters of dye so violently the co-pilot considered dumping the load to save their lives.

Foster pulled back on the reins and all twelve reindeer began to cycle in unison again, an easy trot as they approached terminal velocity aiming for a warehouse roof labeled, TD-12, into which it appeared they would soon crash. The lead reindeer accelerated upwards, the team followed suit and the sleigh leveled off at 500 feet, screaming across the roofs of the manufacturing plants on the other side of the boulevard that separated them from the warehouse district.

"WHERE ARE WE GOING TO LAND?"

Foster climbed up on the bench, held the reins tightly for balance and screamed, "ANY WHERE WE WANT TO!—SLEIGH'S IN DISTRESS! He took the reins in his teeth as they careened above the buildings, illuminated brightly within, and lifting one leg off the bench, posed with his arms outstretched beside him like some ancient elfin god of old.

"WHAT IF WE GET CAUGHT?"

Foster spat out the reins and leapt out into space, curling his body quickly in a mid-air somersault: "WAA-HAA!" he cried as he landed back where he started with both feet.

"CAUGHT? WE ARE TO BE COMMENDED—TOO BAD OUR PAYLOAD'S NOT ON FIRE!"

"WHERE ARE WE GOING TO LAND?"

Foster jumped back down to the bench, "AT MY BROTHER'S PLACE PROBABLY . . . BEYOND THE RUNWAY!"

"WHY?"

"BETTER FOOD, THE REINDEER GET A MINERAL BATH AND WE CAN SELL OFF SOME OF THIS DYE FOR MORE SCHNAPPS!"

"SELL OFF THE DYE!"

"THEY WOULD EXPECT SOME DAMAGED GOODS AFTER A LANDING LIKE THIS! IF THE PAYLOAD'S NOT SCRATCHED THEY'LL KNOW WE WERE FAKING!" Foster grabbed the reins again, gained some altitude and blew over a series of hangars on the far side of the *Reindeer-O-Drome*. As an unlit airfield came into view, he saw an unfamiliar crowd on the tarmac surrounding what looked like a brightly-illuminated box car.

"UH-OH!" Foster cried.

"WHAT?"

Searchlights on the tarmac swung around and caught the pair in freeze-frame just before they flew over the crowd.

"I THINK WE JUST BOUGHT OURSELVES ONE HECK OF AN INTERROGATION WHEN WE LAND!"

"WHAT? WHAT DID WE DO?"

"DIDN'T YOU SEE THE SLEIGH RAILS ON THAT THING?"

"SLEIGH RAILS—ON THAT LOCOMOTIVE? IT CAN'T

POSSIBLY FLY!"

"WELL, IF IT DOES, THEY'RE GOING TO NEED SOME REALLY BRAVE PILOTS TO FLY IT WHO DON'T FAKE ABORTED LANDINGS!"

Foster pulled hard on the reins for braking, and descended to something very close to emergency landing altitude.

"WHAT DOES THAT MEAN?"

"GOTTA MANUFACTURE SOME BRAVERY!"

"WAIT!   I   THOUGHT   THIS   WASN'T   A   REAL EMERGENCY?"

"IT IS NOW!" Foster cried. He jumped down to the floorboards, lifted the Kingpin Inspection Plate and grabbed a woven cord that held a well-lubricated pin. He yanked hard, dislodging it, and rolled over back-first against the bulkhead.

"WHAT THE—?"

"PREPARE FOR IMPACT!" Foster cried.

The team flew away on their own and the sleigh plummeted the last thirty feet to an unlit and ungroomed tarmac at well over a hundred knots.

* * *

"Good God!" Santa cried, "What was that!" He was standing in the darkness with his team of designers beside the massive sleigh they were inspecting. The outliers in the group had bolted to their sleighs and sped to the crash-site.

"It's proof that we have too many sleighs aloft, Santa." Gilliland said. He was foreman of the sleighter project. "It's proof that too many of them are obsolete, with strained harnesses, tired teams and poorly-trained pilots. This is the very reason we've got to get this sleighter aloft now—not next season. Now. We need bigger teams, heavier payloads, fewer flights."

"The tanners are saying that the weight alone of a harness for 108 reindeer is a challenge," Santa said.

"I won't lie to you, Santa. It is. But we have learned about sleighs what the English learned about boats—the bigger they are the more efficient they are to propel."

Santa regarded the prototype before them: it was many times longer and wider than a sleigh. To demonstrate how large it was, the elves had opened the rear doors and crammed as many reindeer as could fit. A total of 74 reindeer intertwined their antlers, stepped on each other's hooves and nipped each other's hind-quarters until they, too, were convinced that this thing could not possibly leave the ground.

One week later the harness was ready.

"HEAVE!" cried Gilliland. "HEAVE!"

The harness was pulled laterally across the ice by a dozen elves and a team of reindeer.

"STRAIGHTEN UP THERE!" Gilliland called. "Bring the ass-end even!"

For the remainder of the day the compliment of reindeer required to fly the monstrosity twisted and sidestepped themselves into place. The attendant elves climbed on their backs, swatted them forward, stayed under-hoof and urged them this way or that. When the elves took their places in the sleighter—three abreast, holding the reins of 36 reindeer each—Santa came out on the airfield to inspect the scene.

He walked along the length of the reindeer teams and across the front of them. As he reached the rear of the teams, all aboard the sleighter eyed him.

"It's never going to fly," one elf whispered to the other.

"Fly?" the second responded. "It will never again move from this spot!"

His tour complete, Santa walked back to the sleighter. "I heard what you said."

Two elves shrunk below the bulkhead. One remained.

"Santa," Cavanaugh asked. "Will it fly?"

Santa turned and walked back to the hangar without answering.

Cavanaugh took off his cap and slapped the elf beside him who was snickering. "You're fired!" he said. "Report to the dung house."

"What?"

"You heard me. Report to Frosted Composting!—and the rest of you, pull up the king pin! Roll up the reins! And get those reindeer out in the same order in which they were put in!"

When all was put away, Cavanaugh sought out Santa in a small office outside of the Planing & Steaming shop alongside the lumber mill. "Santa?" he asked. "Will it fly?"

"Hmm?" Santa looked up from the plans for a new children's stake-bed wagon. "Will it fly?" he asked himself. "It must fly," he answered. "It must fly."

He pulled out of a pocket in his coveralls, a graph given to him last year by the Census Bureau. He laid this before Cavanaugh and pulling a flat red pencil out from behind his ear, pointed to a spot on the graph. "We are here along this gentle slope." He touched the pencil to the graph and made a small "X." "The population of the earth has doubled since I began my work, but the growth was slow and steady. The population should double again in just two hundred years, maybe less"— he touched the pencil lead to graph farther up the curve and hard enough to make an indentation in it—"which means, if what we think is true, then we are to see an explosion in the human population that is unprecedented." Santa pointed to a steep rise in the graph. "The population should double again in just a hundred years after that and then again in just seventy-five and then again in as few as fifty."

"Oh, my God," Cavanaugh pulled off his cap and held it to his chest, his eyes glazing over at the graph.

"The reason I have not shared this with anyone, Cavanaugh, is because there is no need to cause undue alarm. All of this is speculation until we are able to document the projected growth. If it is found to be true, then we are going to be dealing with billions of human beings, do you understand? Not millions. Not hundreds of millions. But billions of them, Cavanaugh. That's why that sleighter is going to fly out there and the sleighter after that and the sleighter after that."

Cavanaugh nodded. "Uh-huh."

"There is an old saying, Cavanaugh, 'liars figure and figures lie.' Do not be alarmed by these numbers. The odds against our succeeding have always been great."

Cavanaugh nodded.

Santa put the pencil back behind his ear.

"The growth in population could be my greatest ally. The geometric growth in the number of people living on the earth could bring with it a geometric expansion of their souls and peace may come to them on their own without my having to wait until absolutely every single human being finally believes in me—like that reindeer of old, I will simply be able to lead them to the precipice, and they'll take that final leap of faith themselves."

Cavanaugh nodded again. His eyes watered. He did not know what to say. But then he saw it! In his mind's eye! A system of pulleys and cables he would install in Sleighter Hangar Number Two! The entire harness was to be suspended above where the reindeer were to be assembled with the reins already in place running through them!

He rushed out of Santa's office without so much as a good-bye. The following morning the newly-christened sleighter was dragged back into the hangar. The reindeer were marched in, too, and jostled into place. They were instructed to lean their heads back until they could feel the tips of their antlers on their flanks. The harness came down slowly and was laid upon them. Eighteen elves worked from back to front, buckling, fastening, pulling and prodding, unhooking the guy-wires and tightening everything fast.

Cavanaugh jumped up into the sleighter, grabbed the left-most reins, signaling to Millman and the elf between them to do the same. He called out to the pilot in the first row, first team, portside to take the teams forward. The sleighter moved as the teams progressed from the half-step to full. Cavanaugh and his assistants called out to each of their three teams to tighten up, stay in line, steady their pace. The sleighter moved out onto the extra-long airstrip designed for it and taxied a full half-mile to the end. Cavanaugh pulled the team far to the right on the bulb-shaped terminus of the runway and made a U-turn that was so slow, so wide, and so cumbersome, that the team jack-knifed and the lines fouled.

Cavanaugh sat down on his bench, closed his eyes, rubbed his face and listened to Millman give the orders this time. He imagined himself somewhere else. He thought about that penciled X. When he looked up, the team was straight as an arrow, aiming straight down the runway. The reins were taut. The reindeer stood tall with the antlers held high. Two hundred and sixteen branches of antlers poised at the ready.

"PILOT!" Cavanaugh called to his lead reindeer. "TAKE YOUR TEAMS OUT ON THE QUARTER-STEP. BRING THEM TO TAXIING SPEED ONLY, AND SLOW TO A STOP AT THE FAR END OF THE RUNWAY."

Cavanaugh felt his response in the reins.

"QUARTER-STEP!" Cavanaugh called and the sleighter moved ahead slowly, steadily, amid the rhythmic percussion of four hundred and thirty-two reindeer hooves drumming the ice beneath them. He looked up over the bulkhead where the harnesses terminated, behind the teams of "The Engine Room"—where the biggest, strongest, most muscular, reindeer were harnessed.

The ice slid beneath their rails.

"Thirty-five knots," Cavanaugh said to himself. He thought he felt a chatter in the sleighter rails and pulled back on the reins for greater speed to see if he could eliminate it. The chatter only became more pronounced. He stared back over the side.

"MILLMAN," he called above the growing wind. "ESTIMATE OUR SPEED!"

Millman lifted his head up and his cap flew off revealing a bald and shiny head. He looked to the rear of the sleigh and looked back at Cavanaugh. "FORTY-FIVE, FIFTY?"

Cavanaugh nodded in agreement. He looked over the side again at the rails trembling now in concert with the vibration he continued to feel.

We are either approaching take-off speeds or we are about to break apart, he thought.

He looked over toward the sleighter hangar, beyond it to the whole *Reindeer-O-Drome* Complex and then forward to the fast-approaching end of the runway. He surveyed the nine-teams of undulating reindeer, and the field of condensation they created above them with their breath. He thought of Santa, their talk together and the population curve that viciously shot upward on the graph . . .

"GET UP!" he cried and pulled hard on the reins for acceleration. *"GET ON UP!"* Millman and the other elf joined in. The sleighter surged forward. The vibration grew more pronounced. Cavanaugh braced himself between the elevated footrests and the sideboard before signaling for even greater power as the groomed path of the runway disappeared into the snowy crust of the Arctic. He snapped back on the reins for rotation. In an instant the first three teams were up, their hooves silent, cycling freely in the cool Artic air. The next three teams curved up to follow their brethren, then the final three. With a sharp jolt and then silence—the massive craft was airborne at seventy-three knots.

Cavanaugh signaled the pilot for a steep climb and continued to pull hard for continued acceleration. The teams reached 1,500 feet at 110 knots and Cavanaugh signaled to level off. The teams responded. Cavanaugh turned his head sideways to listen for any signs of distress from the teams or the sleighter. He felt for any vibration on the bulkhead, but there was none. He ducked behind a lone pane of lead crystal attached to the bulkhead to escape the slipstream and pulled back on one rein, peeling off easily to his 10 o'clock. He dove back down toward the compound. Two hundred knots, two-ten, two-twenty.

The craft was stable, he thought.

Two-thirty, two-thirty-five . . .

Does this thing have a top end?

Two-forty, two-forty-five . . . Cavanaugh pulled up at five hundred feet and aimed for the green-houses where, he believed, Santa would be experimenting with a brand new strain of mint.

Their shadow, solid at the sleighter, and speckled throughout the teams, sped along the Claus Compound below them, instantly turning greens to gray, reds to rust, beiges to brown before returning everything it touched to its original color in the brilliant intensity of the Arctic sun. The shadow of the sleighter dove down subterranean air vents and painted itself darkly up walls before slicing toward a roofline and undulating across great expanses of corrugated tin. It wrapped every object exposed to it in momentary darkness and removed pearl essence instantly from ten thousand pupils of dolls waiting to be wrapped.

Their shadow advanced from building to building extending itself to twice its length as it covered the distance between them. It dove down through the skylights of the greenhouse, leaving an outline on its many-mildewed panes—but falling deeper into the building itself, it served, momentarily, as a false night upon that which was ruled by the sun. Each leaf, each shoot, each tendril within the building registered darkness as quickly as it was perceived, and multiplied the sensation thousands of times over in the dense vegetation of its artificially-heated home. Without any quiver, or retraction, or closing, or folding, every plant life signaled an abeyance of photosynthetic creation, and Santa, sensing something had changed, looked up.

The shadow painted his face in darkness, hollowing cheeks filled with a never-ending feast. It returned pigment momentarily to the follicles of his cheeks and head that had been robbed of their color long ago. It eliminated the profile of jowl, gut and thigh and bathed him the cool forgetting of ten hundred years of work. He stood in the image of his own young manhood, staring upwards into the heavens in expectant discovery. The sleighter shadow permeated his flesh, and finding the never-ending muscle of his might pumping steadily within him, warmed it with the intensity of the very sun that it now hid from view. A great dark smile broke across his face as he recognized overhead the sensuous dig, pull and throw of reindeer in motion.

"HO! HO! HO!" he called out and grabbed his belly. "HO! HO! HO!" he called out as the sleighter's shadow passed over and he was bathed in illumination once more. "HO! HO! HO!" he called out as he was blinded briefly, and was forced to look away from the glass ceiling to the black and blue blinking of the plants emerging from the over-exposure of his eyeballs. "HO! HO! HO!" he called out to the plants themselves which, in the span of two-and-half seconds, remained motionless, but sensed in their greenery all that had transpired before them.

Chapter 9:
The Curse of the Suburbs

"Santa?" Inman asked. "What do you make of this?" The Chief Elfin Mapmaker reached up and handed Santa a swirled drawing on parchment. They were in Santa's study perched above the millworks behind the *Reindeer-O-Drome* flight school.

Santa spun it around in a number of directions. "What is it?" he asked.

"A suburb," Inman replied. "Llewellyn Park, Orange, New Jersey."

"A suburb?" asked Santa. "In Jersey?"

"No, *New* Jersey, Santa. North America. The United States. Construction is well underway. We couldn't even count the number of plots."

"Over a hundred?" Santa asked.

"At a minimum."

"A suburb in Jersey, I could understand," Santa said. "England is crowded. But in the United States?"

"In the State of New Jersey."

"Hmm," Santa intoned. He spun on his swivel chair and spread the map on his desk. "England's first suburb—Clapham Commons, I believe—proved to the English that traditional suburbanites—thieves, forgers, fortune tellers—wouldn't encroach upon developed lands."

Santa adjusted his reading glasses. "If anything, it forced these people back to the city center—where the money is—and left these homes alone . . . "

"Inviting more to be built?"

"Unfortunately, yes."

"To think that a merchant would ever want to leave the safety and permanence of an urban area is preposterous! He would have to return there to work anyway! Why would you have one building in which to work and one in which to sleep—IMPOSSIBLE!"

"I can't understand it either, Santa," Inman said, as he took off his visor and rubbed his small head with his free hand. "I thought Park's Village would go under and the other one—Victoria . . ."

"Victoria Park," Santa said.

"Victoria Park—yes," Inman said. "But both flourished."

"And now this . . . across the pond."

"Yes."

Santa handed the sketch back to Inman and dismissed it entirely. "It is the aping of architectural fashion," he said. "The Americans won their independence from the British and have envied them for it ever since."

"Yes, sir," Inman replied.

"You will recall that the Dutch alarmed your forebears when they erected their first windmill—had them fearful that they would slice up our teams on Christmas Eve as they proliferated all around the world," Santa said. "Very few of them now remain. We made do with that threat—we shall make do with this one, too."

"I hope so."

"Human beings," Santa continued, "were not meant to live in rows of spaced-out boxes. Since time immemorial they have either lived in complete isolation: the farmhouse, the hunting blind, the outpost, or igloo; or they have lived in great density—the village, the tribe, the town, the city. The very success of their social institutions was predicated upon a great suffocation of the masses—think of Ancient Rome! Think of Greece! Think of Egypt, for God's sake!"

"Santa, are you trying to convince yourself this is not a threat?"

"No, I'm trying to convince myself that all the world should be as Manhattan!" Santa exclaimed. "What is wrong with wide streets, tall buildings, and everything built in a grid? Yardless brownstones make short work of Christmas Eve deliveries, Inman."

"I understand, Sir."

"Or a farmhouse, beside a lonely country lane!" Santa stood up from the desk and walked across his office warmed by a pot-bellied stove fueled by the broken toys leftover from Christmas Day. "I'm in and out in seconds, Inman. Seconds!"

"I understand, Sir."

"This construction in the suburbs is merely a fad," Santa said. "A passing fancy!"

"If you say so," Inman said.

"It's...it's just a trend," Santa said and then built up his fire with broken toys he remembered playing with.

* * *

At Inman's retirement party, he pulled Santa aside. "I've given my son all the files."

Santa was trying not to spill the cider in his teacup as he was dancing, to the extent Santa was capable of dancing. "What files?" asked Santa.

"The suburban files." Inman said quietly.

"Inman, you're retiring! Leave it alone!"

"I'm not retiring, Santa." Inman said. "You won't let me work anymore."

"You can barely see."

"And I think you are the one who is blind!"

"To what?"

"Suburbia." Inman said. "Islands of homes in Riverside, Illinois. Inconsistent shapes with twenty, thirty, forty suburban homes each—easily more than a thousand plots all told."

Santa stopped dancing. "A thousand?"

"Over a thousand, with a hundred homes built already and every one—every single one—is set back from the street and separated from its neighbor by a yard. Their roofs are too small to land on and their gardens too cluttered for take-off. Each would have to be approached from a street that was some twenty or thirty paces away."

"TWENTY OR THIRTY PACES AWAY?" Santa exclaimed? His teacup trembled on the saucer he held.

"My son, Paul, has all the files."

"MY GOD!" Santa moaned. "I wish this were *my* retirement party."

"There is a bright spot."

"What?"

"The developer is running into some trouble."

"Superb!" Santa said. "What kind?"

"The gamut—an economic downturn, some embezzlements, lawsuits . . . the usual."

"Bravo!"

"But the families who have moved in *love* their homes."

"What is our Census Bureau saying?"

"Christmas is doomed."

* * *

Santa stood before The Map of The Known World once it was updated with Inman's analysis.

"The red pins represent the existing suburbs, is that correct?" Santa asked.

"Hm-hmm," said Mrs. Prs., Executive Director of Santa's Census Bureau.

"And the yellow pins represent the ones being built?"

"That is correct."

"What is the forest of trees over here represent?"

"The green pins represent the planned communities approved for construction by the prevailing local municipalities."

"THE WHAT?"

"Those are the suburbs that about to be built."

"JUST LIKE THAT?" Santa cried. *"OVERNIGHT?"*

"They're very popular," Mrs. Prs. explained. "In fact, to own your own suburban home in the United States is called 'The American Dream.'"

"THE AMERICAN DREAM?" Santa roared. *"THIS THING IS THE NIGHTMARE OF THE NORTH POLE!"* He wrapped his arms around himself, and then unwrapped them and ran his hands through his hair.

"I'M GOING TO NEED A TRACK TEAM TO DELIVER TO THESE THINGS!" he cried.

"Maybe you will," Mrs. Prs. responded. "In a hundred years, the vast majority of this country will live in housing such as this."

"GOOD, GOD!" Santa said, as he fell into the chair behind him. He reached into the zippered pocket of his coveralls for the maple bar he had left there yesterday and peeled it away from the lining.

The Suburban Task Force Commander, McGuigan, stepped before him with a report three inches think. "It's unstoppable, Santa. Without some kind of intervention from you, the world will be turned into one huge suburb."

"Intervention?" Santa asked between bites. "What kind of intervention?"

"Deny Christmas gifts to the children of the developers," McGuigan offered.

Santa raised a finger to his lips, considered his proposal for a moment and then dismissed it entirely. "No, no," he said. "That won't do."

"The essential problem as we understand it," McGuigan said, "is the gross inefficiency of it all--one stop per house at two-point-eight children each."

"And what about the sleighters?" Santa asked.

"Oh, yes," McGuigan said, turning toward the serpentine path of a suburban roadway map on display to his right, "Sleighters are a problem. They simply will not be able to land in suburban developments to refuel your sleigh with gifts."

"Do you mean to tell me that I'm going to have pack in all the gifts myself—one sleigh-full at a time?"

"We would certainly hope not, Santa." McGuigan said, staring still at the map and the pattern of pins upon it. "And yet there will be few streets straight enough or long enough or wide enough for the sleighters to land in. As yet we haven't quite figured out where we can reload the sleigh once it enters the suburb."

"How quickly can you build a scale model of a development like this—something with precise elevation and lighting."

"Six months," McGuigan said.

"Six months?" asked Santa.

"If you want precision, yes. Six months, maybe five," said McGuigan.

"Five?" asked Santa.

"O.K., four-and-half months from today and it will be perfect, but no sooner."

"Fine. But I want it to be complete—automobiles, trees, telephone poles . . ."

"It will be perfect."

"Very good."

Two weeks before the deadline, Santa was lead into the newly-christened Suburban Task Force War Room in complete darkness. The windows to the room had been blacked out from what little sunlight was afforded them that late in the year. His guide, Willy, one of the model-builders, guided Santa using a small flashlight, holding it low to the ground. Willy stopped Santa from progressing any farther, and clicked the light off.

"Welcome to Flambeau Terrace," McGuigan's voice could be heard in the darkness. "A planned development of three hundred and forty-two custom built homes."

Slowly before Santa's eyes, thirty-eight miniature streetlights illuminated a subdivision 25 feet square.

"With five modern floor plans to choose from," McGuigan continued, "and a palette of distinctive coordinated colors, we of McGuigan Development Companies—a subsidiary of The Red Man Real Estate Group, Inc.—invite you to explore the home of the future and discover how truly affordable it can be!"

"Beautiful!" Santa clapped his hands together. "It's marvelous—I mean, *terrifying!* Are those electric lights?"

"Yes, they are." McGuigan reached down from where he was sitting and illuminated the houses from within, block by block. "Battery-powered."

"Very nice." Santa walked around the table. "And these dimensions are correct—the streets, I mean?"

"Santa, this thing is accurate down to the very last dirt clod. The subdivision that we copied was buzzed by our sleighs every night for a month this spring."

"Why would someone build a street to nowhere?"

"You mean the cul-de-sacs?"

"Yes," Santa said. "I can understand if you are building out at land's end, but why would take a perfectly good parcel of land and create a maze out of it?"

"Everyone wants to live on court, Santa," said McGuigan. "No traffic, few neighbors. The rest of the world is completely out-of-sight."

"What is so suddenly wrong with the rest of the world?" Santa asked.

"I don't know," McGuigan replied. "But this entire subdivision sold out within weeks of the model home being finished. We will be delivering to it just two months from now."

"Good God!" Santa said. "Give me a world of avenues!" He studied the development in miniature and remained silent for a moment. "What is with all this netting here?"

"That would be the . . .uh . . . the power lines, Santa."

"Power lines?" He asked. "Criss-crossing the street at odd angles?"

"The very height of efficiency, sir."

"So no real estate grid on the ground means no electrical grid in the air?" Santa asked. "All the power lines are chaotic?"

"Evidently," McGuigan said. "It's another one of our issues. Our biggest challenge, though, is that there is no rhyme or reason to the direction or curve of the streets. There is no way to land in the middle of one these developments and deduce which street will lead you out. It would also appear that there is some distinction given toward developers whose designs are most maze-like."

"God, help us!"

"Every single subdivision will have to be mapped and routed and learned."

Santa shook his head in disbelief. "Let us proceed, McGuigan. Give me 3:15 AM somewhere in North America with ground fog and a couple of the street lights out."

"Starlight?"

"No."

"Any precipitation?"

"No, but make the streets wet."

"Turn up the second valve, Will—there to your left," McGuigan instructed his assistant. "Ground fog coming up."

Small water sprinklers in the artificial lawns spread a fine mist across the handcrafted gardens, and upon the small strips of volcanic rock beside the driveways and then on the walkways, sidewalks and streets themselves. There was a plop of dry ice into a tank of water beneath the subdivision and, slowly, small wisps of vapor emerged from the miniature sewer grates, manhole covers, and fire hydrants valves throughout the silent neighborhood. The lights dimmed in the houses to the level typical for an early morning in winter and three of the streetlights flickered and then went out.

McGuigan handed Santa a pointer with a scale model of his reindeer team and sleigh on the end of it, and for the remainder of the morning Santa flew touch-and-go's into and out of the suburb, charting his progress, requesting occasionally for a change in lighting and weather.

The following day Santa brought in the Steerage foursome of his own reindeer team, three of his best sleighter pilots and his Chief of Elfin Logistics and staff.   They listened to McGuigan present the evidence once more for the impending growth of suburbs, reviewed the projections of their expansion throughout the world and spent the entirety of the afternoon working with models of sleighs and sleighters, reindeer and elf to see how they could possibly deliver gifts more efficiently in light of suburban constraints.

They ended the meeting in complete disagreement.

The sleighter pilots wanted approval to build disposable sleighters that would be flown in heavy and hot to the suburbs for a controlled crash landing on the short, poorly-lit surface streets. Their teams would be unbuckled and flown away individually, while the elves were left to off-load the gift onto Santa's sleigh and break down the sleighters into manageable sections to be flown out by the elves and their reindeer.

The elves on the other hand wanted to increase their presence on the ground tenfold, to limit the use of sleighters on Christmas Eve, and to pack in all of the gifts with their own squadron of sleighs.

The only idea tendered by the reindeer was to fly into the model home at high speed and impale the real estate agents on their antlers—"I think that would do it!" cried Chaney, newly-appointed navigator of Santa's team.

None of these were acceptable to Santa, least of all the continued joking at the expense of the real estate agents and their lenders. He looked over at McGuigan, sighed, and said, "Let's begin again tomorrow."

In the morning, Santa summoned McGuigan to his study overlooking the *Reindeer-O-Drome*. "McGuigan," he said. "These things are impenetrable—the suburbs. Is there not one developer who understands my plight?"

"There might be one."

"One I could talk to?"

"I think so," McGuigan said. "There is one person who realizes what this sprawl will do to our delivery schedule. He just built a street in his subdivision to send the message to you in flight that he understands."

"A street?"

"It's in the shape of a heart."

"For me?"

"Uh-huh. It's not visible from the ground, Santa—it just looks like another court. And it's too small to be recognizable from altitude—but if you are coming in low on Christmas Eve, you will see clearly it's been designed in the shape of a heart."

"Where is this?"

"San Bruno."

"Serra San Bruno? In Calabria?"

"Wrong continent. The *City* of San Bruno—on the San Francisco Peninsula—California—the United States."

"The City of San Bruno?"

"The City with a Heart!"

"Evidently," Santa said. "But how would I land on a heart?"

"He built a landing strip specifically for you—a short street that leads right to it. Can't miss it—Cupid's Row!"

"For me?"

"He wants to make sure you can land there. He doesn't want you to ever forget San Bruno. Or the children who live there."

"Who is he?"

"Unsin."

"Interesting name."

"Mmm."

"Can you go visit our Mr. Unsin? Can you tell him our situation? We need to tour these housing developments ourselves, talk to the people who build them and get their permission to train within the confines of an actual subdivision."

"WHAT?" cried McGuigan.

"I mean what I said."

"But, your policy—your . . . *your covenant*."

"My policy to have no daily contact with humankind will have to be bent on this occasion. I do not think such contact, if performed with the dignity of our office and our aims, will in any way affect our ability to perform our work."

"Well, what would you have me do?" McGuigan asked.

"Tell Mr. Unsin I need a training ground to fly into. Tell him I need an actual subdivision to practice our landings, a place with consistently bad weather, poor lighting, and possessing an absolute maze of streets. Tell him to find me a dead-end to fly into."

McGuigan shook his head.

"Oh, and another thing—we'll need a car."

"A what?"

"A car, McGuigan. An automobile."

"Where in the name of God am I going to find you an automobile?"

"Ask Unsin," Santa said, taking off the eyeglasses and wiped them on his sleeve. "I'm sure he'll know."

"Mother of God!" McGuigan said, bringing his small hands to his face and rubbing it.

"McGuigan, I gave similar instructions ages ago to your ancestors and they returned to me with King James and his bride, Louise—the very first reindeer to fly. Each age has its own struggle—you are now embroiled in yours."

"I understand," McGuigan said finally, "I'll do as you ask."

Chapter 10:
Gee, Our Old LaSalle Ran Great

Ten days later McGuigan burst into Santa's study out of breath, "GOOD NEWS! BAD NEWS!" he cried.

"Good news!" Santa said.

"We've got a car!"

"Great!" cried Santa. "What's the bad news?"

"We've already had a collision!"

"A collision? Where?"

"Sleighter Hangar 12—we crashed into the very same sleighter we had just unloaded it from."

"Let's go!" Santa jumped up, grabbed his cap and followed McGuigan down the narrow stairway leading from his study.

McGuigan held open a trap door to the frozen catacombs at the end of the stairway and the two of them climbed down into an underground passageway that ran diagonally across the compound. They emerged within the hangar, hearing the shouts of elves, the braying of reindeer and the flatulent backfire of a combustion engine in distress. They ran to the open hangar doors in time to see a beige and brown four-door sedan spin past them in circles at twenty-seven miles an hour—one, two, three, four complete spins on the slick ice of the tarmac as the rear tires whined in the futile search for traction.

"NOT ON THE ICE!" Santa cried as he ran after the car. *"NOT ON THE ICE!"*

"TURN OFF THE IGNITION!" McGuigan cried, in fast, short-legged pursuit of Santa, *"TURN IT OFF!"*

Santa caught up with the car sitting silently beside the runway. "Who's driving this thing?" Santa asked, as he looked in the window.

"I am," an elf poked his head up from beneath the dashboard.

"And so am I," another elf beside him peered up at Santa.

"Would you be so kind as to extract yourself from this contraption, harness up a team of reindeer to it and tow this thing back up into the sleighter?"

The elves nodded in obedience.

McGuigan caught up to Santa, "Can't run on the ice, huh?"

"No, no, no! They can't run on ice at all!"

"Well, I didn't get an instruction book with it. How do you like it?"

"Very nice." Santa stood back and admired it. It was a shiny beige box of a car, with dark brown fenders and running boards. It had wide white wall tires and two covered spares set in the front fenders. It had two large headlights set in front of a tall tombstone radiator. The two-bladed, chrome bumper was crushed into the fender on the passenger side where it had rammed the sleighter.

"It's a LaSalle," McGuigan said. "It has the best of everything!"

"What did it cost you?" Santa asked.

"A sleighter-full of lumber," McGuigan said.

"A SLEIGHTER-FULL OF LUMBER?" asked Santa.

"Yes, why—is that too much?" McGuigan asked.

"I don't know," Santa said, "What do these things normally go for?"

"Oh, about a sleighter-full of lumber!" laughed McGuigan.

"HO! HO!" laughed Santa. "Very well then. Where'd you find it?"

"Cheap Pete's Car Land!"

"Any trouble?"

"More than I care to recount."

"And how about our developer?" Santa asked.

"He directed me to one town over—a new subdivision that's just breaking ground. Looks like a bad one."

"And did you meet that developer?"

"Even better!"

"What?"

"I met the mayor!"

"The mayor! That's terrific!"

"I don't know, though, Santa. He's kind of ambitious."

"So am I. When do we meet him? Where does he live?"

"South San Francisco, and he wants to meet soon."

"The Mission District?" Santa asked, visualizing a meal of Irish victuals.

"No, no, no. The *City* of South San Francisco."

"Oh, the *City* of South San Francisco—yes, of course. When do we leave?"

Chapter 11:
Rendezvous at The Old Guard

The La Salle spun its tires as it made a left onto Grand Avenue. A downshift went badly, and the engine struggled with too high a gear, jerking its way through its intended firing order until it died in an explosive blast of carbon.

"Clutch in!" McGuigan called from the back seat. "Brake on! First gear—make sure you're in first. Find neutral and double-check! Good, now, starter . . . STARTER ONLY! Don't touch the choke. Good. Ease out the clutch—brake off—gently with the gas now, gently. Good . . . give her a little more . . . don't be afraid to wind it out. Good. Clutch in, gas off, pull down into second—very good—clutch out gently—good—gas now, a lot of gas, get us up over the hill. Very good." McGuigan leaned back into his seat next to Santa who was slumped down away from his window with a black fedora pulled down over his eyes.

They passed City Hall.

"How are we doing?" Santa asked, peering out the side window.

"We're almost there," McGuigan said, "Look!" He pointed out the window at a large sign planted in the earth. "Coming This Fall! The Old Guard. 245 Discriminating Homes for the Discerning!"

The La Salle came to abrupt halt, with its engine still running.

"The road has ended," called one of three elves at the controls.

"Pull up into the dirt very slowly, cut the engine and put on the brake."

The elves did as they were told and the five of them sat there quietly for a quarter of an hour.

"Still think this was the right idea?" McGuigan asked.

"I do," Santa said, nodding.

A car drove up from behind them and cut its engine. McGuigan stood up on his seat and looked out the back window. "Ford," he said. "Coupe—could've got one of those. I think this is our guy."

Santa rolled down his window as a trim, middle-aged man with his hair parted neatly and combed to the side approached the car. He wore a short dark gray jacket with brown trousers. He stepped cautiously through the dirt and bent down to address Santa.

"Mr. Claus?" he asked, "Max Boardman." He extended his hand through the window which Santa had rolled down.

Santa took it, closed his eyes, and held it for a moment. "A toy train," he said, "with a wind-up engine and matching caboose."

"Excuse me?" Mayor Boardman asked.

"What you wanted more than anything else that Christmas that your father went away to war—do you remember?" Santa gripped his hand tighter and patted it with his free hand.

"Why, yes! Yes, of course. It came with its own wooden track . . ."

"A three foot loop." Santa let go of his hand.

"Yes, I could assemble it in the dark—it's just as you say."

"And your, sister, Maria—how is she?"

"Oh, she's great, Santa."

"All grown up."

"Yes, all grown up and married."

"I expect I'll be visiting her household soon."

"Yes, she's . . . she's with child."

"Two of them, I believe," said Santa.

"Really. Twins?"

"If I am not mistaken. You give her my best, won't you?"

"I most certainly will."

"And you've made Mayor, Max?"

"I have, yes, Santa."

"Very good. And I trust you've been informed of the predicament that I'm in."

"I understand it very well." Mayor Boardman looked over to McGuigan and greeted him with a nod, "Mr. McGuigan."

"Mayor," McGuigan greeted him.

"Well, why don't we go for a walk," Santa suggested. "Is that all right with you?" Santa asked McGuigan.

"Quite all right. I'll stay here with the boys."

"Very good." Santa climbed out of the car as the Mayor held the door open for him and then closed it. Santa adjusted his fedora and his trench coat and clasping his hands behind his back, walked alongside the Mayor up the hill.

"My deliveries, Max, are based on tradition. I deliver to the very families in the Old World that I have been delivering to for five or six hundred years—some go back that far. The same cobbled streets, the same thresholds, the same fireplaces. My reindeer, who inherit the routes from their fathers and their fathers before them, fly to these places on feel. They are familiar to them on their first visit by the inherited memory of the undying reindeer race.

"But these new lands that are being built . . . there is nothing to intuit about them. There is no tradition to them. There is no history. They are the creation of happenstance. They are the whim of a builder crafty enough to buy the land cheap, and smart enough to entice people from the city to buy the homes that he builds upon it.

"You, yourself, grew up on Fillmore Street—did you not? A beautiful, wide, straight street and lived side-by-side with your neighbors? Fillmore Street did not turn and twist in upon itself to convince its residents that they live in some remote part of the world—"

"I know, I know—it must seem crazy to you."

"No, crazy is not the word. Crazy I reserve for war—like the one your father served in, or for hatred or violence of any kind. This is simply exasperating for me. I risk my entire operation by coming to you like this, but I am afraid that without some cooperation from people who are to learn the nature of my operation intimately, I am not going to be able to keep up with the demands that are put upon me each Christmas."

"And that's where I come in."

"That's where you come in—yes. McGuigan has assured me that you are about to break ground on the most logistically-hideous subdivisions that we have yet seen—something none of my reindeer could fly into now in the dark."

"Well, I don't know about that."

"Well if the plans are as bad as I've been lead to believe, it would be a perfect training ground for us."

"Well, I've given all of this a lot of thought and I've talked to the developer about what I want to do and he's in agreement with me. Our plan to keep your work secret is to limit knowledge of your arrival to as few families as possible—I would say 25 or 26 maximum. All of them would be screened by me personally for suitability and would live along a one block airstrip that butts up against this outcropping here," Mayor Boardman held his hand out to unusual mound-shaped hill before them rising 250 feet in the air. It appeared to Santa to be the upturned bill on a baseball cap of the larger mountain behind it.

"I'm assuming you would come in over the bay, having flown down the coast and come through the gate. You would fly inland at Burlingame, south of the airport and go west to the El Camino Real . . ."

"Highway of the King," Santa noted.

"That's right, Highway of the King. You would make a 90 degree turn and head north—actually northwest—through Burlingame, Millbrae, San Bruno and pass the racetrack en route to South San Francisco. You would make another 45-degree turn, more or less, and bear down directly for the airstrip. You would have to clear a row of houses at the very end and drop down quickly to land. With this hill at the end of a 300 foot cul-de-sac, you'd have almost no chance to go around."

"And the weather?"

"Consistently bad. You've delivered to the older homes farther north, but this land is trapped in a valley. The San Bruno Mountains are to our East, and the Santa Cruz Mountain range is on the coast. The ocean is so close to us on the other side of the range there, that they've named an entire town after the ocean herself."

"*Pacifica!*" exclaimed Santa.

"Yes, Pacifica. The end of the world for us. Set upon cliffs and in a narrow valley inland, she receives the worst of the weather, but she cannot contain it all. The fog overtakes her and rolls up over Skyline Boulevard and then breaks over that range there," the Mayor pointed up to the hills to the West. "And then it rolls down in slow motion to cover us here. It's a wet fog that sticks to the ground and has nowhere else to go."

"Perfect!" said Santa. "But I don't like the airport."

"I didn't think you would. The planes are noisy and smelly but they're here to stay . . . over every city, in every nation . . ."

"I'm painfully aware of that."

"But I have a plan. The reindeer have an excellent sense of smell, do they not?"

"Very good, yes."

"If you can bring them in right above the water, I can guarantee to always keep them on course south of the airport."

"How?" asked Santa.

"I am talking to two chocolate-makers in San Francisco, the Ghiradellis and the Guittards, about moving their factories down here by the bay, right where you would come inland. Your reindeer could vector in on smell with their eyes closed."

"Hmm," said Santa. "We always had a problem hiding our chocolate factories in the Old World. Couldn't keep the smell down."

"Well, you still can't, Santa. And I guarantee you even in a storm, I will make the shoreline smell like hot cocoa when you are coming in for a test flight."

Santa nodded. And then thought for a moment. "If it's as foggy as you say on our base leg, Max, how will we know to when to make our final turn on the approach?"

"Yes, I've given that some thought, Mayor Boardman said. "I'm talking to Charlie See—you must remember him . . ."

"Mm-hmm," Santa replied. "And his lovely mother, Mary."

"That's right."

"And his young bride, Florence."

"Quite right," Mayor Boardman responded. "I am speaking to him about opening a candy factory on the El Camino right where you would make your turn. It could serve as a beacon for you..."

"...for reindeer noses!"

"Exactly, right," Mayor Boardman said. "Landing lights wouldn't work at your height in the fog and the local citizens wouldn't think twice about Charlie cooking up a late-night batch of fudge."

"I see."

"We could break ground quickly to get that first exhaust flue operational."

"And the airstrip?"

"We'll grade this week and pave the next. It will be yours as long as you need it. With any kind of cloud cover at all, you could fly in at high noon and not be noticed."

"But 300 feet?"

"It's a little bit longer actually," Mayor Boardman responded. "But McGuigan did say that you wanted to practice some suburban landings that would make your hair stand on end."

"Stand on end, but not fall out!"

"It will be built at good incline, Santa. You'll be landing uphill."

"Hmm," Santa intoned, looking up at the hill before them. He then turned around and looked out toward the El Camino. "A candy factory in the middle of the suburbs, Max? Wouldn't that be a...a tip-off?"

"I'll...uh...I'll mix in a little light industrial around it," Mayor Boardman said. He moved his hands around in front of him as though mixing some imaginary ingredients. "No one will notice. Big chain link fence. Keep Out signs. And we'll paint it something non-descript— make it look like a hospital."

Santa did not respond.

"No one will think twice," Mayor Boardman said. "They'll drive right by it—trust me."

"I guess that could work," Santa said.

"I think you'll find everything in South City will suit your needs."

"You've obviously given this a lot of thought."

"I have, Santa. I'm going to help make this a great city. One of the best in California. We are The Gateway to the San Francisco Peninsula. We have our own harbor, and, as we discussed, an ever-expanding airport in our backyard."

"You have a lot to be proud of."

"We do. But it's hard to be compared to San Francisco all the time."

"I can imagine."

"The City Council just approved my idea to put up a sign up on the backstop to your new landing strip—Sign Hill, we're now calling it. I want to put up something like HOLLYWOODLAND down south, except set in the ground in large block letters. Maybe 'SOUTH SAN FRANCISCO, CITY OF THE FUTURE' or 'SOUTH SAN FRANCISCO, CITY OF COMMERCE!'—Something like that."

"Sounds terrific," Santa said, "as long as it doesn't read 'SOUTH SAN FRANCISCO, SANTA'S PROVING GROUNDS!'"

"Oh, no, Santa," Mayor Boardman replied. "Mum's the word. Everyone involved in this—the developer, the builder, the residents, the City Council—will proceed in absolute secrecy."

"It sounds very well thought-out," Santa said turning around and peering now at the fog creeping in from the coast. "McGuigan will let you know what our thoughts are."

"Very good, Santa."

"Probably, next week or so."

"Whenever you're ready."

"Good," Santa said, as he shook Mayor Boardman's hand one last time. "And this landing strip, Max," he said, as he turned away. "Do you have a name for it?"

"I do." The Mayor nodded. "Lilac Lane."

"Hmm," intoned Santa, as he adjusted his fedora. "Lilac Lane." He walked by himself back to the car. "Quaint."

Chapter 12:
South City

"South San Francisco?" Chaney asked, stamping the ice off his hooves. "You mean like China Basin?"

"No," replied Reader-Speeder, assistant to McGuigan.

"Lake Merced?"

"No."

"The grasslands of Colma?"

"No."

"Hunter's Point? Potrero Hill? McClaren Park?"

"No, no, none of those."

"Candlestick Point?"

"No, no, no, the *City* of South San Francisco!" Reader-Speeder exclaimed.

"The only city south of San Francisco that I've ever flown to is Brisbane," Chaney responded. "Those views!"

"And Daly City!" called Sutcher, co-navigator to Chaney, from the other side of the stall in which Chaney was being groomed.

"Right!" Chaney admitted his error. "Daly City to the southwest and Brisbane to the southeast!"

"Well, no—I mean, yes, that's true; but this is SOUTH San Francisco."

"Let me ask you a question, Reader," Chaney asked leaning his head over the pony-wall beside him and looking down at the elf directly.

"Does the border of the City of San Francisco actually touch the border of the City of *South* San Francisco?"

"Well . . . I. . . " Reader-Speeder looked down at the straw-covered ice of the reindeer stalls.

"Answer the question," Chaney demanded. 'Yes' or 'no'?"

"I..."

"Answer the question!"

"No."

"Well then, that settles it. I'm not flying to a city named south of a city it isn't."

"But it is *south* of San Francisco!" Reader-Speeder protested.

"Listen, Reader, three-quarters of the Known World is south of San Francisco, for Santa's sake! How can you expect me to find a city whose fathers have named it incorrectly?"

"But it's easy to find," Reader exclaimed. "It's just south of the San Bruno Mountains!"

"Then why isn't it called South San Bruno?"

"Or South San Bruno Mountain!" Called Sutcher still unseen.

"Because it's North of the CITY of San Bruno, of course."

"North of San Bruno?" cried Chaney.

"Yes!" said Reader-Speeder.

"South of San Bruno Mountain?"

"Yes!"

"Not touching San Francisco?"

"Yes!"

"WE'RE NOT GOING!" Shouted Chaney and Sutcher together, laughing with a high-pitched reindeer whine and kicking the stall between them loudly, until they collapsed into their beds of straw, refusing defiantly to fly that day.

Chapter 13:
The Riddle of Refueling

"OPEN THE DOOR!" Chaney said, his head lowered, his brow points touching the chest of the panting, dirty little elf, Russell, who had raced between his legs, and stood at the door to 23 Lilac Lane.

"DON'T DO IT!" another elf cried—this one was flat on his face on the porch with the hoof of the reindeer behind Chaney driven into his back.

"TURN THE KNOB!" another reindeer cried, with an elf in his antler branches who had stopped struggling, but was trying to kick him in the eye.

There were mob of reindeer and elves struggling on the porch, crammed up against the front door. They had raced from the landed sleighters with the elves far in the lead across the open, undeveloped land, until the reindeer had been let loose from their harnesses and had raced past them up the Lane only to discover the doorknobs were made exclusively for humans.

Russell looked past the crowd to the open windows across the lane. There were antler branches visible in all the second-floor windows. The reindeer had taken over.

"I'll let you in, Chaney, but you need to lower your points," Russell said between breaths. "You let them down, and I'll turn the knob and concede."

"DON'T DO IT!" the elf on the ground cried. "Oooh!" he cried as a reindeer applied more weight.

"Just let those crown points down nice and easy."

Chaney complied slowly as Russell hopped up and caught him by his antler roots, pulling himself up on Chaney's head quickly and then pushed off the knob with his rubber-soled heels, turning it. The door burst open and the reindeer stampeded the model home with Russell technically in the lead, feet first, inverted, holding onto both antler branches for all he was worth as Chaney spun in the entry hall, spied the stairs and bolted for them. He slammed his antlers on opposing walls of the stairwell trying to dislodge a determined Russell who groaned each time he was punched through the plaster.

The pair reached the landing, and Chaney, feinting first towards the second bedroom, tried to whip his head around—but Russell let go before he could, landed on his feet and then ran into the master bedroom, his little arms upraised.

"DARLING, IT'S OURS!" Russell cried. "OUR BRAND NEW HOME!" He burst out laughing.

Staggering into the room, Chaney galloped over to the far wall of the master suite—the one with the laundry chute in it, lifted his leg and sprayed a pungent yellow arc across the wall. He threw his head down and stumbled across the wall-to-wall olive shag.

"I was looking more for a split-level, anyway," said Chaney, smashing a sconce with his antlers. "And the kitchen's too small."

* * *

"STAND BACK...FARTHER BACK. BEHIND SANTA, PLEASE! ON THE LAWN AT LEAST," the Lane Traffic Controller called to Santa and the assembled *Reindeer-O-Drome* Flight Instructors in the darkness.

"WHAT LAWN?"

"OK—THE DIRT!"

"Sleigh 72 on the approach, Santa. Passing over See's Candy . . . NOW!"

"I can't see anything."

"Neither can they."

"FIVE, FOUR, THREE, TWO . . . *LIGHT UP!*"

Lilac Lane exploded in brightness, as twenty-five thousand bulbs strung along the rooftops illuminated the block-long cul-de-sac.

"RIGHT ON TIME!"

Out of the gloom, the lead pair of reindeer sped furiously

downward. They paused, and cycled backwards when they saw how close they were to The Lane—but it was too late, it would be a hard landing. They raced forward again.

The team crashed down on The Lane. Half a shoe went spinning over the spectators' heads and the sleigh rails exploded in sparks when it first hit, as the two elves in control of the sleigh pulled back hard on the reins for braking. The reindeer rushed on to the end of The Lane, over the sidewalk, and through the shrubbery where it looked like they would meet their end by crashing into house number 42, but its façade split neatly down the middle and swung open, exposing the phony front to the only house on The Lane not yet built. The teams tore through what would have been the front room, entry hall, kitchen, rear bedroom and bath.

All the landing lights on the houses were extinguished and The Lane was enveloped in darkness.

"A little . . . ah . . . fast, don't you think?" asked Santa.

"Oh, a little. And that was with an unloaded sleigh."

"Can you slow things down?"

The elf got on the phone to the warehouse at See's Candy. "Norm, we've got to ease up on this next team. Send them in at seventy knots . . . what? . . . I don't know—milk chocolate means eighty—wait, I've got the list right here." He reached in his back pocket for an envelope folded in half on which he had written the Candy Landing Codes. "Send up butterscotch for seventy. Clear the vents with vanilla first and go with butterscotch." Turning toward Santa. "OK. All set."

Santa searched his pockets for something to eat.

"FIVE, FOUR, THREE, TWO . . . *LIGHT UP!*"

The lead reindeer burst through the cloud cover out-of-line with The Lane. The elves on board pulled hard on the starboard reins for braking to correct the drift and tried to accelerate the port team, but they were too close to the ground to adjust. Crabbing as they did in the air, the right rear sleigh rail extended far into the path of the observers.

"JUMP!" cried the Lane Traffic Controller.

Santa and his observers leapt into the dirt, face-first upon the empty trenches where the sprinkler systems were to be installed. The sleigh's rail sliced the air just above them.

The lead reindeer touched down in a sprint, the sleigh fishtailing behind as a sleigh rail hit hard and cracked in two. The wooden sleigh slammed into the street, ground over the curb, and plowed through the dirt of lot of house number 38 where it tore down a plywood cut-out of the landscaping that was to be planted there.

"Maybe we could just *mail* the kids their presents," one elf lying on the ground whispered to another. They covered their mouths so that no one could hear them laugh.

But Santa did.

* * *

McGuigan stood beside Santa outside the sleighter hangars early one morning two weeks after the time trials at Lilac Lane had concluded.

"One minute more," Santa said, looking at his pocket watch.

"One minute more for what?" asked McGuigan.

"You'll see," said Santa, still concentrating on his watch.

Santa looked off to the east. "There," he said. "Look."

A sleighter was on the approach of Runway 12 A.

"What am I looking at?" McGuigan asked.

"Just a second," Santa said, tracking the progress of the sleighter. "There," he said. "Behind them."

McGuigan strained his eyes. Flying low behind the sleighter—but gaining on them—appeared to be Santa's own team of twelve.

"Your sleigh?" asked McGuigan.

"Mmm," Santa intoned. "Now watch this…ten, nine, eight…"

As the two teams approached the runway, their flight paths converged, and the sleigh, flying below the sleighter pulled up directly beneath it.

"What the…?" asked McGuigan.

"…seven, six, five…"

The sleigh was flying just above the deck when the elves of either craft began barking orders to each other from above and below.

"…four, three, two…"

The pair was to pass just in front of the hangar when two doors from the belly of the sleighter opened up and a short stub of a chute emerged.

"What in the world…?"

"ONE!" Santa called out.

As the two flying ships passed directly in front of the pair at seventy knots, the sleighter dumped a sleigh-load of packages into the hold of the sleigh below it, which dropped toward the ground as it received the full weight of the gifts. A dozen or so packages missed the sleigh entirely or bounced out of it and disintegrated upon impact with the runway. The sleighter peeled off hard to eleven o'clock, retracting its chute and closing its belly doors as the sleigh pulled up in a steep climb to starboard.

"What was that?"

"HO! HO! HO!" laughed Santa. "That, my good McGuigan, is the very latest in mid-air suburban refueling techniques."

"WHAT?"

"I'm going to have these sleighters fly in heavy and hot to the suburbs—come right in across the deck after I've delivered my gifts. I'll jump back up in the air with my sleigh—the nearest sleighter hits me and—*POW!*" Santa punched a gloved fist into the palm of his other hand. "—I get my gifts and slam down on the next street to unload again!"

"You are out of your mind!"

"It's going to work!"

"Do you realize the split-second timing that all of this would depend upon?" McGuigan exclaimed. "—AND IN COMPLETE DARKNESS?"

"I certainly do," Santa bent down and adjusted the lapels on McGuigan's coat. "And I'm sure your group will make short work of it."

McGuigan didn't speak. He didn't move from the spot. He then called out to Santa as Santa crossed the hangar floor to the wind tunnels beyond, *"THIS IS IMPOSSIBLE!"*

Santa nodded in agreement, but did not turn around.

McGuigan shook his head. "It's impossible," he repeated to himself. He walked out onto the smooth frozen runway to examine the remains of the gifts that had exploded upon impact. "It can't be done."

* * *

"Santa," McGuigan asked, "Do you know the difference between fog and mist?"

"Yes," Santa said. "My spectacles never get foggy!" He slapped his knee. "heh! heh!" His oak office chair seemed to creak in agreement.

McGuigan did not laugh.

"I presume you are about to tell me the difference," Santa said.

"Visibility," McGuigan said. "The difference is merely visibility."

"Fog is a cloud on the ground," McGuigan said. "It is preceded or appointed by mist. Sometimes it is absent owing to the proxy of mist."

"Wherever there is water you will find both," Santa said.

"And our continents are mere islands, and nearly all ground is moist."

"Do you know the foggiest places on earth?"

"The Grand Banks, certainly—" Santa said.

"Newfoundland, yes," McGuigan said.

"And for second place there is Po Valley in Italy..."

"Or Ebro Valley in Spain . . ."

"Yes," said Santa. "But for the absolutely downright foggiest, I would switch continents and say Point Reyes in California—not too far from Lilac Lane."

"Nearly two hundred days of fog per year!"

"With only a lighthouse for us to deliver to!"

"And those few houses that are going up."

"But not a city!"

"No, not a city—which is my point," McGuigan said. "Hard to sell houses in the fog."

"Splendid!"

"Except if you're a cagey real estate developer."

"What?"

"What do you think of delivering to Pacifica further south?"

"Challenging."

"New homes are now being built there on a street called Sunshine Drive!"

"WHAT?"

"Sunshine Drive!" McGuigan said. He pulled the street sign out of a sack and held it up. "And you know what the developers told prospective home buyers about the fog?"

"What?"

"That it would all burn off once the nearby shopping center was built!"

"They didn't say that!"

"The said that the heat from the operation and all the traffic associated with the shopping center would burn off the fog!"

"And the home-owners believed them?"

"Bought up every lot! This on a street so foggy that kids are not allowed to play outside until their parents can see to the other side of the street! THE OTHER SIDE OF THE STREET!"

"I've never actually seen sunshine in Pacifica," Santa said.

"It appears long enough to illuminate sales contracts for new tract homes and dry the ink once new home owners have signed," McGuigan said. "And then the fog rolls in."

"Well, we'll just show up and tell them the truth—they'll listen to us!"

"What? You and me? The Yuletide Tub o' Lard and Munchkin Man!"

"Hey!"

"We're just going to show up and staple a CONDEMNED notice on a few thousand homes?"

"We could do it at night! Ho! Ho! Ho!"

"Santa, there is an allure these builders have toward water that troubles me—they draw home-owners—*they draw us*—right into the thickest of fog belts."

"Hmm."

"There is a town in Southern California—I kid you not—which will soon stretch twenty-seven miles long and only a half-mile wide along the water!"

"I don't believe it!"

"Well, maybe three-quarters of a mile wide!"

"You're pulling my leg."

"Everyone wants a view!"

"Of water? What's to see?"

"NO PEOPLE!"

"People want a view of *no people*?"

"People want a view of *no subdivisions*!"

"Then why do they build them?"

"To get away from people!"

Santa shook his head.

"It gets worse!"

"That's not possible!"

"There is a new subdivision outside of St. Louis that has made-up canals!"

"What?"

"Pretend canals full of water to build houses on!"

"That's not true!"

"I've been there!"

"They dig a trench and fill it with water!"

"That's not true!"

"They fill it with water so the houses that sit next to it will be worth more money!"

"Worth more money?"

"BECAUSE IT HAS A VIEW OF NO PEOPLE!"

Santa shook his head. "That's not possible!"

"Do you know what the real estate developers put over these canals?"

"I'm afraid to ask!"

"BRIDGES!"

"What?"

"BRIDGES!"

"You mean they dig a canal to pour in water to place a bridge where there used to be dirt?"

"YES!"

"MCGUIGAN, YOU'RE MAKING THIS UP—YOU'RE FIRED!"

"THANK YOU, SANTA!"

"YOU MAKE UP IMPOSSIBLE STORIES—"

"AT LEAST I'M NOT A DEVELOPER!"

"—TO TORMENT AN OLD MAN!"

"YOU KNOW WHERE THEY STORE THE BRIDGES?"

"WHAT?"

"DO YOU KNOW WHERE THE DEVELOPERS STORE THE BRIDGES BEFORE THEY PUT THEM OVER THE PRETEND CANALS?"

"Where?"

"ON DIRT!"

"WHAT?"

"THEY SHIP THE BRIDGES IN! STORE THEM ON DIRT! DIG THE CANALS! FILL THEM WITH WATER! BUILD THE HOMES! INSTALL THE BRIDGES! AND THEN ENTICE FIRST-TIME HOME-OWNERS TO DRIVE *OVER* THE BRIDGES *ACROSS* THE WATER AND *INTO* THE HOMES—"

"—THAT DON'T LOOK AT PEOPLE!"

"YES!" McGuigan cried. "THAT DON'T LOOK AT PEOPLE!—

THAT COST MORE MONEY PRECISELY BECAUSE THEY SIT ACROSS MAKE-BELIEVE CANALS AND DON'T LOOK AT PEOPLE WHO, FRANKLY, DON'T WANT TO LOOK AT THEM!"

"Oh, my aching head!" said Santa. "Oh, my ever-suffering brain!" Santa rubbed his temples, and then reached into the pockets of his coveralls for something to eat, but finding nothing scraped shortbread cookie crumbs under his nails.

"You can't reason with these people, Santa! You can't woo them with toys! They'll grow up anyway and extort each other! That's what they do for a living! They charge each other too much for homes, too much for automobiles, too much for milk, too much for puppies—"

"They don't charge for puppies!"

"—they charge TOO MUCH for puppies, Santa! Too much! They charge too much for puppies, too much for toothpaste, too much for underwear!"

"Yes, yes, I know!"

"Children work like slaves in buildings that collapse to sew buttons on the tuxedos for rich men a world away!"

"I know! I know! I've seen it!"

"You're not enough, Santa." McGuigan put his hand on Santa's arm. "You'll never be enough. The reindeer are stupid. They are goats made gullible by ambition!"

"But look at what I have done!"

"Kept alive a patient who should have died ages ago?"

"Look at the progress!"

"For people for whom murder is *news*!"

"You know the effect I have had!"

"Effect? In a place where soon there will be more guns than people?"

"Don't remind me."

"Santa, there may be mist on your spectacles but there is fog in your eyes!" McGuigan said. "It can never work!"

"But my reindeer!"

"They are suicidal!"

"My sleighter!"

"Obsolete at launch!"

"My complex at The Pole!"

"Soon to be discovered, I'm sure, and then you'll be forced to tunnel underground!"

"And the developers?" Santa asked.

"Carving up the earth one spadeful at a time to fool the young into spending a lifetime paying for the paradise of a fog-filled illusion! A fog-filled illusion that you fly reindeer into at high-speed!"

"BOOM!" a terrific explosion rocked Santa's workshop, knocking plastic figurines of himself to the floor.

McGuigan rushed out of the room without a word, slamming the door behind him.

Santa turned in his chair to his desk. *Probably the glue factory,* he thought. *Or that new boiler in confection.*

He pulled off the white gloves he had been wearing to study the spotted skin on the back of his hands. He turned them over to see if he could read within his palms the certainty of his success. His creases did not please him.

"I am the man called Claus," he reminded himself. "I am Santa Claus, the all-giving, ever-living fixture in every child's heart. I cannot be stopped. I must move forward. My success is inevitable. I shall subdue the entirety of the earth. I will push back all fog and every darkness. I will encroach upon the heart of humanity one child at a time. All are to hear my message. All will listen. Nothing can stop me. I possess an army of elves and an air force of reindeer, who cut concertina wire with antler tines, repel bullets with hollow-haired hide, defuse land mines with hooves split for the very purpose, and drown out the cries for battle with the jingling of little silver bells that call all to Christmas!. While I have life within me, I shall create! While I have raw materials at my disposal, I shall produce! While one boy dreams of me, while one girl stays up late to look for me, I shall endure, I shall succeed, I shall conquer! Have I ruined one day of the year for these people? I have nearly ruined two! Soon it shall be a week, then a month, then a year, then all time, then I shall rest, then I shall retire, but not until then, not until the manifestation of my will—*mine!*—*me!*—*Santa's!*—is complete!"

McGuigan rushed back in the room. "IT WAS THE BOILER IN CONFECTION!"

"Build three more."

"What?"

"Build three more."

"And tell Patolli and Parcheesi to move forward with that game."

"What game?"

"That board game."

"The one you loathe?"

"It will be a huge success this season."

"The one you cheat at?"

"Yes."

"MONOPOLY?"

"I want a first printing of a million sets."

"YOU REFERRED TO IT AS 'THE GAME OF HATE'!"

"It will be all right," Santa said. "We'll use play money this time . . . just like those bridges."

McGuigan shook his head and then brought his small hands to his face. "Oh, my God!" he said.

"We all like to pretend, McGuigan," Santa said. "We all like to play." He stood up from this chair and arched his back to stretch it. "Put your faith in make-believe."

The End

The site for South San Francisco was selected by G.F. Swift and purchased by Peter Iler of Omaha in 1890 for the establishment of stockyards and a market place for cattle. Needing money, the pair became allied with Chicago capitalists and formed two joint stock corporations, one named South San Francisco Land & Improvement Company, the other as Western Meat Company. The name for South San Francisco followed the pattern planned by G.F. Swift, whose company had taken over the Western Meat Company, as his other plants were named "South Chicago" and "South Omaha." The city was incorporated September 19, 1908

From www.ssf.net